Papazoglou, Orania

Once and always mur

Once and Always Murder

Once and Always Murder

ORANIA PAPAZOGLOU

A CRIME CLUB BOOK

Doubleday

NEW YORK   LONDON   TORONTO   SYDNEY   AUCKLAND

A CRIME CLUB BOOK
PUBLISHED BY DOUBLEDAY
a division of Bantam Doubleday Dell Publishing Group, Inc.
666 Fifth Avenue, New York, New York 10103

DOUBLEDAY and the portrayal of a man
with a gun are trademarks of
Doubleday, a division of Bantam Doubleday Dell
Publishing Group, Inc.

Library of Congress Cataloging-in-Publication Data applied for.

ISBN 0-385-24843-1
Copyright © 1990 by Orania Papazoglou

For
MICHELLE TUMASH
who brought the cat

Great virtue consists of a strictness in small things.
  —LOUISA HALDORAN CAMPBELL MCKENNA

If my mother ran the universe, Theodore Roosevelt would have been immortal, and he'd still be President.
  —PATIENCE CAMPBELL MCKENNA

Once and Always Murder

ONE

THERE IS NO TRAIN STATION in Waverly, Connecticut. There may
have been once—there's a small section of town called Waverly Depot
—but for as long as I have known the place, it has been deliberately
isolated from all modern forms of transportation. Even the roads are a
joke. 202, 45, 109: square white markers with those numbers on them
appear at irregular intervals along the two-lane blacktops that twist
and dip and rise and plummet through the hilly landscape, remnants of
a time when the mere presence of asphalt spelled "progress." When
the snows come, the town is cut off, not only from the towns around it,
but from the access roads that lead to the interstates that lead to the
stores that make living in the country possible. Waverly has no super-
markets, no groceries, no convenience stores, no malls. Shopping for
food means a forty-five-minute trek to Waterbury. Shopping for clothing means a longer trip—to West Hartford, where the West Farms
Mall has branches of Lord & Taylor and Laura Ashley and Ralph
Lauren Polo, or into Manhattan. Waverly does have a hardware store,
and a few gas stations, and the best bookstore in the state of Connecticut. It also has a great many very old houses. Some of these houses are
very large and very expensive: reconstructed New England antique.
Others are very small and not expensive at all. The people who live in
those will sell you cordwood in the winter and shovel snow off your
gravel drive at twenty dollars an hour. At least, they will do these
things if they can get out of their own driveways and down the road to
yours—which they can't, most days. The snows always come, and with
them some of the nastiest patch ice in the known universe.

There was a lot of patch ice that first day of February, stuck in the
hollows at the bottoms of the hills, glowing black and wicked at the
worst spots in the curves—but, believe it or not, it wasn't what I was
worried about. For one thing, it had been long enough since the last
heavy fall—nearly two weeks—so there wasn't a lot of snow clogging
the road. For another, I'd had the sense, back in New York, to rent

not a car but a Jeep Wagoneer. Four-wheel drive, oversized snow treads, and a brand new set of chains conspired to make me feel secure, except when I did something stupid and nearly flipped us over. The Wagoneer is not a vehicle that tends to flip over, but the people who designed it hadn't taken into consideration either Litchfield County or me. Litchfield County is bad enough. I am a disaster. One of the reasons I moved to Manhattan in the first place was that it was possible to live there without ever having to drive myself anywhere.

Actually, the reason I moved to Manhattan was that I didn't want to spend my life in Waverly, Connecticut. Like millions of other young women in millions of other small towns, I had my eye on the exciting, the adventurous, the cosmopolitan—the not-home. That I grew up rich instead of poor, and went away to boarding school instead of being imprisoned in the local high, mattered not at all. Boredom is in the eye of the beholder. I was as agonizingly stupefied by tennis parties and high tea as my best friend Phoebe was by sock hops and the Dave Clark Five in Union City, New Jersey.

Of course, Phoebe could go home to Union City and know not only that she had changed, but that the city had changed right along with her. Waverly never changes. I was bombing along on 109, through a landscape that looked exactly the way it had when I was eight years old. The same houses were in the same places. The same side roads wound out of sight into the same hills. The longer I drove through it, the worse I felt. It was as if my life for the past ten years—or maybe the past twenty—had been an illusion. I hadn't really lived any of it at all. Now I was waking up, and as soon as I shook the sleep out of my eyes I'd find I'd turned into the person my mother always wanted me to be: married to a nice stupid man from a good New England family, traveling to Fairfield twice a week for the meetings of my charity boards, obsessional about gardening.

I brushed hair out of my face and reminded myself I was none of that. I did live in Manhattan, and the man I was marrying was from anything but "a good New England family." He had grown up poor, and Greek, three blocks from Phoebe's mother's kitchen. Stuffed in the back of the Jeep, I had the paraphernalia of my authentic existence: copies of all three of my published true-crime books and the working notes for my fourth; a copy of the new maintenance agreement for my apartment on Central Park West; my adopted daughter's first shot at a "real" short story. I even had a few clippings from the

New York Post—LOVE GIRL DETECTIVE SCORES AGAIN—as if, all else failing, I could prove who and what I was by the blithering absurdities of Rupert Murdoch's successors.

I caught the glint of ice just as I was making the turn off 202 onto 109, tried to downshift, and realized I'd been traveling in first gear since Watertown. The wheels spun. The Jeep shuddered and rocked. My stomach disintegrated. Then the miracle occurred for the fiftieth time, and we were on the road and traveling serenely forward once again.

I looked across at the passenger seat and saw that Phoebe had gnawed a hole in the cover of a paperback novel called *Rage for Passion, Cry for Love*. Phoebe was what I was worried about. I was worried about her physical condition, because she was seven months pregnant. I was worried about her mental condition, because she was in the most irrational mood I'd ever seen anyone in, anywhere. Most of all, I was worried about her emotional condition. I have known Phoebe (Weiss) Damereaux for twenty years, ever since we were both freshmen at Greyson College for Women. I have known her poor: living in a three-room railroad flat on the Lower East Side, with a bathtub in the kitchen and the electricity off for lack of payment. I have known her rich: royally ensconced in a ten-room apartment ten blocks north of my own, surrounded by velvet furniture and two-thousand-year-old Chinese snuff bottles. I have even known her triumphant: according to *Publishers Weekly,* she's "The Most Important Writer of Historical Romance Since the Death of Georgette Heyer." This was the first time I had ever known her *insecure.*

She was sitting close to the door, very erect, with her hands folded in what was left of her lap and her face turned to the window. Her best coat, six hundred dollars' worth of Calvin Klein tweed, had fallen off her shoulders and settled near the small of her back—although it was cold in the car, she hadn't bothered to pull it more tightly around her. Her thick wiry hair was anchored to the top of her head with butterfly hairpins. The collar of her Brooks Brothers turtleneck looked too tight. The navy blue wool of her maternity jumper was beginning to strain a little in the chest. In one way, she looked exactly what she ought to look like, pregnant: a four-foot-eleven-inch, naturally plump Santa's elf, surgically attached to a hot-air balloon. In another, she looked like nothing I'd ever thought possible: a Cheshire kitten, maybe, with homicidal tendencies.

On every side of us, there were trees—bare black summer ones and thickly needled evergreens, denuded rose bushes and dispirited hedge shrubs—and the remains of that last heavy snowfall. It was eleven o'clock in the morning, but the sky was gray and thick with clouds, and the temperature couldn't have been much above twenty. Even with the Jeep's heater going full blast and layers of shirts and turtlenecks and sweaters and jackets hanging from my shoulders, I was freezing.

"You ought to put that coat on," I said. "You're going to get sick."

Phoebe wiped fog off the window with the flat of her hand, pressed her nose to the glass, and looked out on an outcropping of rock coated with ice.

"I'm not cold, Patience. You wouldn't be cold either if you'd put on a little weight."

I sighed. Then I reached into my jacket pocket, found my cigarettes, and got one out. I am six feet tall, and have been since I was fourteen years old. I weigh a hundred twenty-five pounds—a weight I reached at twenty and haven't been able to overcome since. Telling me to gain weight is like telling the Ayatollah Khomeini to make sense. And Phoebe knew it.

The dashboard lighter popped and I lit up, keeping one hand on the wheel at all times. My brother George can drive without ever seeming to touch the steering wheel, but my brother George is coordinated. I am a one-woman accident factory.

I took a drag on my cigarette, put it into the dashboard ashtray, and pointed to a narrow access road that disappeared into the hills at our right.

"George and Kathy live at the end of that," I said. "Maybe we'll go up and cook them dinner some night next week."

"You're not going to have time to cook anyone dinner, Patience. You're getting married."

"Is that what this is all about? Now you've decided you want David to marry you?"

"No."

"What is it about, then?"

"Nothing is about anything, Patience. You're imagining things. You've just got bride's jitters—"

"I do not have—"

"—and you're projecting all your nervousness on me."

"Right," I said.

"Besides," Phoebe said, "you couldn't cook dinner for anybody even if you wanted to. You can't cook."

There was a turn I had to pay attention to, so I paid attention to it. Slowing down, I saw a small gray cat run across a field of snow and dissolve into a stand of pines. Waverly, Connecticut.

"Look at this place," I said. "It could be an exhibit at the Smithsonian Institute."

"There's a turn up there, Patience. If you don't do something, you're going to run right into that whatever-it-is."

That whatever-it-is was a roadhouse, and Phoebe was right. Just ahead of us, 109 came to an abrupt end, at least as far as going in *this* direction was concerned. I pumped the brake and pumped the gas and pumped the brake—in all the wrong places, naturally—and nearly spun us into a ditch. When we finally came to a halt, just beyond the stop sign, we were stretched almost diagonally across the road.

The seat belts locked. Phoebe bit her lip.

"Sorry," I said.

"Don't be sorry," Phoebe said. "Drive slower."

"I'm only doing about twenty miles an hour."

"You're going like a jet plane," Phoebe said. "I've never been in a car going so fast in my life."

I closed my eyes and counted to ten. *Phoebe's pregnant,* I told myself. *Her hormones are all screwed up. Be patient. She's always been patient with you.* I opened my eyes again and stared into the roadhouse's parking lot, as if it could tell me something.

"Listen," I said, "would you, by any strange chance of the imagination, want to drive?"

"I don't have a driver's license, Patience. You know that."

"You want to get out and walk?"

"What are you *talking* about?"

"I'm talking about the fact that you've been driving me crazy ever since we left New York. What's *wrong* with you?"

"Nothing's wrong with me."

"Horse manure."

"I *hate* this place," Phoebe said. "Did I ever tell you that?"

I stared at her. "No," I said. "You never did tell me that. I tell you *I* hate it. You come up here more than I do, for God's sake. You spend more time with my mother than I ever did."

"Oh, I like your mother all right."

"So what do you hate?"

"This *place*. This *town*. Waverly, Connecticut."

"Waverly, Connecticut," I repeated.

"Money, money, money," Phoebe said. "Even the air smells like money."

I got my cigarette out of the ashtray and took another drag. "Phoebe," I said, "make sense. You've got to have more money than ninety percent of the people who live here. Your last book did eight hundred thousand copies hardcover."

"Eight hundred sixty-five. I know how much my last book did. And that's not the point, Patience."

"What is the point?"

"There are *kinds* of money, Patience."

"Kinds of money." I stared at the tip of my cigarette. It was growing a long column of ash. "I can't believe this," I said. "I really can't believe this."

"Everybody in this place has had money forever," Phoebe said. "Everybody. And your mother's house is going to be full of people—"

"Including Amelia and Lydia and Tempesta and Ivy—"

"I don't mean those people. I mean your relatives. Your Aunt Cordelia. Your cousin Elizabeth."

"My Aunt Cordelia is an idiot," I said. "And my cousin Elizabeth is a twit."

"She's a *debutante* twit."

"You're having a nervous breakdown because you were never a debutante?"

Phoebe waved smoke away from her face, stubborn. "And now there's this bookstore," she said. "I can just imagine what it's like. It's not like I'm coming up here for a nice quiet weekend and your mother's car is picking me up in Waterbury and I'm going to spend a couple of nights eating Chicken Kiev and—"

"Phoebe." I took a deep breath. "What's wrong with the bookstore? You've never even been in this bookstore."

"I know what it's like, Patience. Trust me."

"Meaning what?"

Phoebe made a face. *"Intellectual,"* she said. "The kind of place they don't even sell romance books."

There was a pick-up truck coming in behind us. I eased my foot off the brake and maneuvered the Jeep into a left turn. It wasn't a very good left turn, but I didn't hit anything, and I only slid about half a foot. The road we were on now was wider and better maintained than 109, so I shifted into second.

"This bookstore," I said, "is called the Chestnut Tree. It's a very nice place run by very nice people, some of whom I've known forever."

"Out here, everybody's known everybody forever."

I ignored her. "I don't know if they carry romance books," I said, "because I've never checked, but I do know they carry your books, and put them right up front, because I've seen them. So you see—"

"Patience, I sell more than anybody in the country except Stephen King. They have to put me up front."

"If you can't be rational, you can at least be consistent. If you're making them money, they can hardly hate you. And they wouldn't hate you anyway. Besides, I can't spend two weeks with nothing to read. Especially not these two weeks."

"Most women enjoy planning their weddings, Patience."

"Most women don't have my mother planning them for them. The day before yesterday, she called me at three o'clock in the morning to tell me tea roses weren't in season this month."

Phoebe stared straight out the windshield. "Your Great-Aunt Felicia is coming," she said. "Your mother told me so."

"Ah," I said.

"You can hardly call your Great-Aunt Felicia an idiot, Patience. Or a twit."

Just ahead of us, the road was abruptly ending again, this time in front of a small gas station. To our left, the brick facade of the Chestnut Tree curved like the outer rim of a boomerang, bordered by a tiny parking lot and a collection of well-kept shrubs that flowered pink in warmer weather. Phoebe was right. Nobody could call my Great-Aunt Felicia an idiot or a twit.

I made a left in front of the gas station and another left into the parking lot. "Listen," I said, "if that old bitch gives you any trouble, just tell my mother. She's been looking for an excuse to murder Felicia for years."

TWO

ONE OF THE REASONS my parents continued to live in Waverly—instead of moving down to Greenwich, say—was that Waverly wasn't a divided town. Down on the Gold Coast, the demarcation between rich and poor is a thick stone wall. The rich have their own schools, their own stores, their own parties, their own clubs. They talk to each other, and no one else. Born rich in Greenwich, you could reach adulthood without ever having come in contact with anyone who made less than a quarter-million a year, and with all your illusions intact. Of course rich people are better than poor people. Of course there's something *special* about you, just because your daddy went to Yale and your mother never looks at the price tags when she shops at Coco Chanel.

In Waverly, rich people send their children to public grammar schools, right along with everyone else. By the time I was twelve, I not only knew everyone in town, I knew my limitations. My father might have inherited a lot of money, but I hadn't inherited his athletic talent. If you threw a baseball at me, I was as likely to hit the catcher, or a tree, as to make it to first base. I might look like a WASP princess, but I didn't know how to flirt, and I wasn't good at putting boys at their ease. Mary Allendar could do both those things, so it didn't matter that her nose was a funny shape and her feet were a little too big. Nothing mattered but performance, and I didn't perform well. For years after I stopped spending time in Waverly on a regular basis—right through boarding school, college, graduate school and the start of my career as a writer—I cringed every time I went to my mailbox. My eighth grade graduating class put out a newsletter. The newsletter made my deficiencies plain to see. Mary Allendar became Miss Connecticut and then first-runner-up in the Miss America pageant. Jane Alice Carr—daughter of the town drunk—got a scholarship to Radcliffe and a scholarship to the University of Chicago graduate school and then a job as chairman of the history department at

Swarthmore. Kevin Dormer's science fiction sagas sold better than my true crime books ever would.

I got out of the Jeep, slammed my door, and started around back to help Phoebe out. Tommy Dick was just pulling into the gas station across the way, and I waved. He got out of the car, squinted in my direction, and waved back. He looked like a real cop, instead of the rural watchdog the town wanted him to be: six four, two forty, bulked up like an overstuffed grocery bag. He even managed to look dangerous, and at a distance. He had a scar down the left side of his face, a legacy of three tours of duty in Vietnam, that made people think he spent a lot of time in knife fights.

I got Phoebe's door open, held out my arm, and said, "Behave yourself. Those are nice people in there."

Phoebe snaked her head backwards. "Someone you know over there?"

"The town cop. When he was eight and I was five, he buried my legs in the mud bottom at Squantz Pond. I nearly drowned."

"There's no such thing in the universe as Squantz Pond, Patience."

"Out."

Phoebe said "umph," did a little jump action, and landed neatly on the asphalt. Then she looked the Chestnut Tree up and down, back and forth, and made a little grimace. "Don't tell me," she said. "It's a replica of the college bookstore at Vassar."

"The college bookstore at Vassar is in a great big pile of bricks called Main Building." I slammed her door. "And if anybody should feel insecure in this town, it's me. Will you please get moving?"

"If you go in there and buy the new Anne Tyler and four novels by South Americans I've never heard of, I'll never forgive you."

She went clumping toward the main doors. I wrapped my scarf more tightly around my neck and followed her, wondering if that last crack meant I wasn't going to be allowed to buy the new Anne Tyler at all. I wanted the new Anne Tyler. Of course, I wanted some semblance of peace and quiet over the next two weeks even more, so I might be willing to restrict my book buying to the paperback original productions of Lydia Wentward and Ivy Samuels Tree. It was a hard choice.

Phoebe had gone inside by the time I reached the doors. I went in after her, wiping my boots first on the mat on the sidewalk and again on the mat in the vestibule. Then I went into the store proper.

I found Phoebe standing to one side of the doors, looking at the double bookcase that rested against the desk and that was the first thing customers saw when they came in. The case held only hardcover books, only new releases, and only what the store considered especially commercial or especially recommendable. It was February, so recommendable was winning out over commercial. Phoebe's latest was there, among the books on the left side, but everything else in the case was "intellectual" to a fault. There was the new Anne Tyler. There was a novel by Gore Vidal. There were slim volumes by Bobbie Ann Mason, Ann Beattie, Raymond Carver and Alice Hoffman. I winced.

Phoebe folded her arms across her chest. "Well?"

"It's February, Phoebe. You're the only commercial writer I know who comes out with books in February."

"You're doing it," Phoebe said. "You just called me a *commercial* writer."

"Watch out for the cat," I said. "She's climbing your coat."

The cat was, indeed, climbing Phoebe's coat. I'd never been so glad to see anything—animal, vegetable, or mineral—in my life. Phoebe has a near mania for cats. She picked this one up, stroked its long, soft, light-gray fur, and began whispering nonsense in its ear.

I began to look frantically around for a salesperson, any salesperson, even one I didn't know. The Chestnut Tree is a large place, actually a series of rooms, and crowded with sturdy wooden bookcases and broad flat tables. The center room has current hardcovers and current paperbacks and a large paperback classics section that takes up the wall space around the windows that look out on the parking lot. The room to the left has a fireplace and wing chairs and used books in hardcover. The room to the right has children's books and gifts. There are so many nooks and crannies, so many private places, there could have been a hundred people in the store without our seeing even one of them.

I craned my neck for a look at the back passage to the office and was rewarded. Advancing into the store with a pile of books in her arms was Susanna Mars. She was dressed in head-to-toe Laura Ashley. Her fine light hair was pinned to the top of her head in a haphazard way that practically screamed "Bennington College." The books she was carrying were translations from the French. None of that mattered. I had known Susanna since I was six. I trusted her.

One of the books slipped. Susanna caught it with her chin, edged it back onto the pile, and looked around distractedly. She registered Phoebe's existence, and also the fact that Phoebe didn't need any help at the moment. Then she turned to me.

It took a moment, but it finally sank in. "McKenna! Hi! Elizabeth said you were coming home!" She rushed to the front desk and dumped the stack of books on the counter. "Lord, those were heavy. I think they're weighting covers with lead. Anyway, I'm glad to see you. I kept some things aside thinking you'd be in, but Elizabeth didn't really say—"

"What is all this about Elizabeth?"

Susanna wrinkled her nose. "You know Elizabeth. She was in about an hour ago. She gave me a lecture about how the *tone* of this place is *sadly deteriorating.*"

"Then she gave you a lecture about your clothes and offered to recommend a personal nutritionist."

"Naturally."

I turned to Phoebe, still occupied with the cat. "This is a friend of mine from New York. Phoebe Weiss. She writes as Phoebe Damereaux."

Susanna's eyebrows climbed. "Really? That Phoebe Damereaux?" She tapped the bookcase just above Phoebe's novel.

Phoebe blushed. "That Phoebe Damereaux," she said.

"This is Susanna Mars," I said. "We went to grammar school together."

"We went to boarding school together for about a week," Susanna said. "I got kicked out. Do you mind signing books?"

The question was directed at Phoebe, not at me, so I hung back. This was not the reception she had expected, or wanted to expect, at the Chestnut Tree. She didn't know what to do with it. Normally, Phoebe will sign books anywhere, anytime, for anybody. It's all part of being a best-selling *popular* novelist, and if Phoebe knows anything, she knows how to be that.

She struggled with Dignity, and Graciousness, and Playing Hard To Get—all of which she can do fine when faced with a man, but can't do at all when faced with a bookseller. She gave in.

"I'd be happy to sign books," she said. "It's very gratifying to see *Timeless Love* right out front like this."

"Oh, we always put your books right out front. You're one of the few really popular writers who understand English." Susanna grabbed a pen and thrust it into Phoebe's hand. "Start on the ones in the case," she said. "I've got about forty more in the back."

She whirled around and hurried to the rear, a slight young woman with no gray hair and a face full of freckles at the age of thirty-eight.

I waited until she was safely out of earshot and then said, "Well?"

Phoebe grabbed a copy of *Timeless Love* from the case. "Don't lecture me, Patience. The last thing I need right now is a lecture from you."

Susanna really did have forty copies in the back. She put them out on the counter, found Phoebe a chair, and then—because the store was empty and she was in no hurry to start putting out the French novels—pulled up another chair for herself.

"You should have been in earlier," she said. "It's been a McKenna family reunion here all day. Elizabeth. Your mother. George with his little girl. She's very pretty, George's little girl."

"Her name's Andrea," I said. "I have an adopted daughter named Adrienne. It causes a little confusion."

"I didn't know you'd adopted a daughter. You should be more careful about sending your questionnaire in to the newsletter."

"Right," I said.

Susanna laughed. "I know. I never send the thing in either. I don't even read the newsletter if I can help it. It makes me feel like a complete dork."

"Me too," I said. "Sometimes I think everybody but me is either winning the Nobel Prize or having a hundred babies."

"It's more babies than Nobel Prizes these days," Susanna said. "Either that, or something positively weird. Did you know Delia got married?"

"Delia Grantham? You mean Delia's still running the newsletter?"

"Well, it was her idea, wasn't it? I mean, none of the rest of us wanted anything to do with the thing." Susanna plucked at her hairpins, making them looser. "Anyway, Delia got married. Last year. And you'd never guess who to."

"The local brain surgeon," I said. "Or the local motorcycle gang leader."

"We don't have motorcycle gangs in Waverly," Susanna said. "She got married to Damon Rask."

"Damon Rask," I repeated. I'd been thumbing through a book on foreign policy, one of those great doorstop volumes that always seem to have black covers with gold lettering on them. I put it back in its place in the case. "How the *hell* did Delia Grantham meet Damon Rask?"

"He bought some land up here about two years ago," Susanna said. "A great big stretch of it up in the hills behind your brother George's place. And then he got very interested in local government."

"Trying to get a zoning variance?"

"Trying to get a dozen," Susanna said. "And then when Will Marsh was killed—"

"*Our* Will Marsh?"

"No, no. His father." Susanna brushed at her hair again. "Doesn't your mother ever tell you anything?" she said. "I mean, it was a very big deal out here when it happened. In 1988. I know it was a long time ago—"

"My parents were in France most of 1988," I said.

"Well, George should have told you, then. Anyway, Old Will either fell or was pushed down the dry well out on the Deverton place—you know, the one that's been in litigation forever, and nobody knows who owns it. And the state police came in and said it was an accident, and it probably was, but Will was the only holdout on the zoning board and two weeks after he was dead Damon Rask got everything he wanted, so *our* Will is convinced—and after all, Damon Rask is Damon Rask, you've got to admit there's something funny right there, and—"

"Excuse me," Phoebe said. "Who's Damon Rask?"

Susanna and I both turned to her. For the first time today, she looked normal: a little confused, but definitely interested. That was one of the things I'd always liked about Phoebe. She could get definitely interested in anything.

"Damon Rask," I told her, "is a very famous trance channeler."

"A what?"

"A trance channeler," I said. "You know, one of those people who goes into a trance and then some dead person starts talking through him. I think Damon Rask's control is an ancient Egyptian pharaoh."

"You're making this up," Phoebe said.

"She's definitely not making it up," Susanna said. "We've got all his books here. He's written about twelve. And they sell like crazy. And he gives seminars—"

"Seminars?" Phoebe said. "On what?"

"On the great words of wisdom handed to him by Amenhotep the Ninety-second," I said. "How am I supposed to know on what?"

"But who'd go to something like that?" Phoebe said.

"About a thousand people a seminar at three hundred dollars a head," Susanna said. "And no, we're not making that up, either. The man's worth a mint and a half. You should see that place he built out in the woods. Seven million square feet and paid for in cash."

"We got invited to his last book party," I said. "Austin, Stoddard and Trapp held it at Telemetron. We didn't go."

"Good for us," Phoebe said.

"If I'd known Delia was going to be there, I would have gone," I said. "Out of curiosity if nothing else."

"Delia probably wouldn't have been there," Susanna said. "She almost never goes into the city anymore. In fact, she almost never leaves her house. I think she's got agoraphobia or something."

"*Do* you think Damon Rask killed Old Will Marsh?" I asked.

"Nah," Susanna said. "Old Will was kind of a crank, you know that. He'd been on some kick about the Deverton place for years—"

"I remember that, vaguely," I said.

"Everybody remembers it, vaguely. I don't know if anybody ever knew what it was about. Anyway, he was always going out there, poking into things, and this time he poked his head down the well and fell in. Our Will found him about two days later. He knew his father well enough to go out there to look."

"I guess," I said.

"Don't guess," Susanna said. "It's depressing just thinking about Old Will, and *our* Will is crazy, so there's that. Speaking of crazy, your Aunt Cordelia was in today, too. And your uncle, the one with the spats and the tank."

"Robert," I said.

"Robert. Anyway, they were all here. They were all buying books, too, which surprised me a little. I didn't think Elizabeth could read."

"Great-Aunt Felicia reads," I said, "and Elizabeth takes care of Great-Aunt Felicia."

"Your Great-Aunt Felicia usually comes in for herself, which she didn't this morning. Thank God for that."

"Mmm," I said.

"Gold Coast relatives," Susanna said. "I have a pack of them myself. You'd think if they hated this place so much, they'd just stay home."

She slid off her chair and picked up the books Phoebe had put to one side, already signed. She looked tired. Her skin was pale. Her freckles seemed faded. She wedged the books under one arm and smiled, setting off a sunburst of tiny lines at the corners of her eyes.

"You know," she said, "there's a house for sale, on 49, right up at the top of the hill. The one with the big white pillars."

"The one with the greenhouse?" I said.

Susanna nodded. "It doesn't have a lot of land, of course, but there it is. And it's going relatively cheap for Waverly. And it's in walking distance of this place."

"Sounds perfect," I said. "I take it you're trying to buy it."

She had her face turned away from me, her eyes fixed on the yellow legal pad the Chestnut Tree used to record the titles of books sold during the day. She reached out and straightened it against the base of the cash register.

"I was thinking you might want to buy it," she said. "I know you live in New York, and you've probably got your daughter in school there, but lots of people have houses in the country. And you always did like that one."

"That's true," I said. "I liked it even when we were children."

"Finished," Phoebe said.

Susanna turned around and gave Phoebe a great big smile. "Wonderful," she said. "Just let me put these in the back again, and then I can help you two buy some books. Which is probably what you came in here for."

"Damn straight," I said.

"I've got a dozen things under the counter for *you,*" Susanna said. "It's Miss Damereaux I'm worried about." She got another stack of books wedged under the other arm, treated us both to another freckle-faced grin, and went trotting off again.

Phoebe watched her go as if she were a rare species of bird, or maybe a toy soldier come to life. "Don't you just hate it when you say the wrong thing and don't even know why it's the wrong thing?"

I was thinking about something else—my Gold Coast relatives, maybe, parked in my mother's house and waiting to move in for the kill. I had no idea what Phoebe was talking about.

"You didn't say the wrong thing," I said. "You didn't say much of anything."

Phoebe snorted. "I wasn't talking about me, Patience. I was talking about you. All that business about did she want to buy that house. It was the wrong thing."

"Your imagination has been on stimulus overload all morning."

"No it hasn't, Patience. When you said that about her buying the house, she blushed. Bright red. You were looking at the back of her head, but I was looking at her face. Trust me."

"After the way you've been behaving today?"

"She's coming back, Patience."

She was indeed coming back, bouncing between the bookcases like a bright yellow bird. She *did* look tired, but she didn't look much of anything else, and I had every reason to suspect that Phoebe was hallucinating. After all, Phoebe had been hallucinating since we left the city.

Susanna scurried behind the desk, reached under the counter, and came up with a stack of mysteries. "Here," she said. "Julie Smith, Linda Barnes, Joan Hess, Lia Matera, Nancy Pickard, Magdalen Nabb, and a new one you haven't heard of yet. Mickey Friedman."

"You have the Grafton?" I asked.

"F Is for Fugitive. Right over here."

"Maybe I'll write a mystery myself," I said. "Will Marsh will kill Damon Rask and take his place, and nobody will ever know the difference."

Susanna giggled. "Then Delia will kill Will, and it'll turn out she's the rightful owner of the Deverton place, and—"

"Oh for heaven's sake," Phoebe said. "Here we go *again.*"

She gave us both her most imperious Queen-of-the-romance-writers look, and marched off in search of a novel without a death in it.

THREE

ON ANY OTHER DAY of my life, I would have spent whatever time I had alone with Phoebe going over and over the story of the death of Old Will Marsh. It was just the kind of thing I liked, in life and in books. It even had a tinge of the bizarre to it, like a story by John Dickson Carr. On this day, I had my mother on my mind—and when I have my mother on my mind, I can never think of anything else. I had forgotten all about Old Will and the Deverton place, and even about Damon Rask, by the time we were out of the Chestnut Tree's parking lot and on the road again. By the time we got to the Old Canfield Road, I was positively morose. I am always morose when I think about my mother. She makes me feel like a wimp.

To do Phoebe credit, she hadn't gotten so strange she'd forgotten about me. She had started making clucking noises while we were still on 42. Then we got to the turnoff, and the landscape changed, and she got wound up tight. So did I. Back in the 1700s—when the McKennas were farmers, and the house they lived in was a four-room shack with barn attached—the Old Canfield Road was our driveway. Now it only looks like our driveway. It seems to run through our gate, except that our gate is always locked. That's the price of no longer living in a four-room shack. Over the decades, and the centuries, bits and pieces had been added to the original house. What we have now is thirty-two rooms, twenty-four thousand square feet, and a floor plan that looks as if it had been drawn by a schizophrenic on angel dust.

Of course, everybody else on the Old Canfield Road has a very large house, too. This is the part of Waverly where Really Old Families live, rich or not. Restlessness and eccentricity had touched every one of them. In the days before historical preservation societies, what you did with your own house was your own business. The families on the Old Canfield Road had done a lot with theirs. Additions had been tacked to the backs and sides of graceful Federals. Porches had been wrapped around the corners of saltboxes. Third and sometimes fourth floors had been added piecemeal. Nobody could complain that the houses all looked alike—except that they did. In a strange and not quite definable way.

If Phoebe's concerns about money and class had been rational, this was the part of town that would have bothered her most. Instead, it was the part that bothered her least. She recognized it. Since it's the only route to my parents' place, my mother drove her through it at least once a month.

She leaned forward, squinted out the windshield, and pretended to be looking at something. She was really just trying to calm me down—but that was such a normal thing for Phoebe to do, I didn't want to stop her.

"You'd think," she said, "the way that Susanna person was talking, that that old Debenture place would be out here."

"Deverton," I said.

"Whatever. It sounded like just the sort of house—"

"It is. It's just not on Old Canfield directly." I gestured vaguely toward the trees at my left. "It's back behind George's place, too. Or to the side of it. Anyway, it's up there."

"Is it haunted?"

"What?"

"Is it *haunted?*"

I shot her a look. I'm not as good at "looks" as she is, but I can do a fair job when I really put my mind to it.

"You're just trying to change the subject," I said. "And don't tell me we weren't talking about anything. We didn't have to be. You're just trying to take my mind off Mother."

"Somebody ought to take your mind off your mother," Phoebe said. "You can't think straight when you think about her. You get paranoid. You don't make sense."

"Well, that's something you couldn't accuse Mother of doing. Not making sense, I mean."

"*Patience.*"

I got my cigarettes off the dashboard. "Okay," I said. "I'm not babbling about the Deverton place, because I know about the Deverton place. Everybody up here does. And for God's sake, it's not haunted."

Phoebe shrugged. "New England. Big old house. Deserted site in the woods—"

I shook my head. "In the first place, it's not that big. It's just a medium-sized farmhouse with a barn, and it's all falling down. It's got maybe eight, nine acres of land—it had more, but I think the old man sold it off after World War II. Deverton, I mean. That old man."

"And?"

"Well," I said, "one day about thirty years ago, he died. And he left a will, and the will said something about 'I leave all my property to my wife and daughter.' The only thing was, he didn't give the names of his wife and daughter."

"So?"

I smiled a little. "Well, everybody had heard his wife had left him and moved down to Darien. I think that was where she came from. She wasn't local, and she'd left him eons ago, and nobody remembered her name. So the town put a notice in the Darien paper, and *then*—"

"Then? Are you going to do a drum roll?"

"I should. What happened was that two women showed up, but not the wife and the daughter. It was two women both claiming to be the daughter. Their mothers were dead. And then it turned out that old Deverton had gotten married some time back in 1916, *twice in the same day.*"

"*What?*"

"Pretty good, isn't it? The thing is, they couldn't prove who'd gotten married earlier in the day, so they couldn't prove who was the legal wife, so they couldn't prove who the estate belonged to. So they went to court."

"And they're still in court, thirty years later?"

"Actually, they're both dead. Their children are in court."

"Good lord," Phoebe said.

"Nice, isn't it?" I said. "And the really funny thing is, the land isn't worth that much anymore. I mean, it wouldn't be cheap, if you wanted to buy it, but it isn't the fifties anymore. We've got zoning here. The town wouldn't let that land be broken up for a development, and the historical society wouldn't let the house be torn down and replaced with a contemporary palace. And there was a little money, but it's been used to pay the taxes, so there can't be much left. Whoever wins in court is going to end up with a ratty old house they can't do anything with and a lot of unimproved land they won't even be able to farm. It's just like Nick says. Litigation is an addiction."

"It has to be good for something," Phoebe said.

"I don't see what. You'd have to do major renovations just to live in the place. And the historical people would probably insist on a reconstruction, which costs an arm and a leg. And what you get when you're done isn't exactly comfortable, either. Give me redwood modern every time."

Phoebe considered this. "Maybe it's something else," she said. "Maybe there's oil on the property—"

"In Waverly, Connecticut?"

"Or something. Maybe Deb— Deverton buried money in his basement. You know what I mean."

"I know, and I know you're wrong. When we were kids, we used to go out there on Halloween. The hoodier element did a lot of damage. The place has been ripped to shreds, Phoebe."

"Maybe whatever it is is buried on the property somewhere."

"Why? Why would somebody do that?"

Phoebe snorted. "Why would somebody get married twice in the same day? The man was a nut, Patience."

"His descendants are bigger nuts. Phoebe, trust me. It's just one of those things. Everybody got all worked up, and now nobody knows how to back down."

"Do they want to?"

"I don't know," I said.

"I think you're sick," Phoebe said. "I never saw you so-so- I don't know what to call it. So not curious. And about something like this. I mean, for heaven's sake. When Susanna started in about all this, I thought we'd been saved."

"Saved from neuroses about my mother?"

"Exactly."

We had come to that place in the Old Canfield Road where the houses disappear and the gate is in sight. Knowing I would have to get out of the car to unlock, I began to slow up. The last thing I wanted was to go crashing through my mother's split rail fence.

Ahead of me, I could see not only the gate but the long, low lines of the house and the fuzzy-gray surface of the screened porch that stretched across the front of it. Phoebe was right. Odd as it was, the place said *money money money*. Self-confident money.

My mother has always been a very self-confident woman.

I made a face. "Phoebe?" I said.

"I can't get out and open up, Patience. Not unless you help me."

"I don't want you to get out and open up. I just—" I sighed. "Look," I said. "There's another reason I wasn't blithering on and on about what Susanna said. I mean a real reason."

Phoebe looked curious. "You're related to the Devertons? Your Great-Aunt Somebody was one of the daughters?"

"Don't be asinine." We were at the gate. In fact, we were practically through it. I made the Jeep stop, by what seemed like force of will, and said, "Just a minute, I'll be right back."

I got out, opened up, got back into the Jeep, drove through, got out, and locked up again. It felt like one of those rituals I'd endured in Mrs. De Rham's dancing classes. I made myself stop thinking about Mrs. De Rham's dancing classes. They'd been held twice a week at a country club in Greenwich. I'd been carpooled to them. I'd hated every minute of every trip, down and back, and every second of every class.

I got back into the Jeep and told my mind to shut up. This was really nonsense. I must have been all of eight years old at the time.

Of course, after Mrs. De Rham's there had been the "subscription dances"—elaborate parties held twice a year in Manhattan hotels, with everyone present in full formal dress. I must have been fourteen, then.

I got my cigarette, saw it had gone out, and lit it up again. "Just a minute," I said. "Let me catch my breath."

"Concentrate on remembering how to get started again," Phoebe said. "And try to remember, your mother isn't going to kill you."

"Believe it or not, I wasn't thinking about Mother." I fussed with the gears, bucked us a few times, and got us rolling. Slowly. "Look," I said. "Have you ever met Damon Rask?"

"Of course I haven't. I'd never heard of him until today."

"Yeah. Well. I've met him. He's published by AST. I'm published by AST. I've seen him around the halls a few times."

"And?"

I tried to think of a good way to go about this. No use. "Tempesta Stewart wrote me a letter about him," I said, "saying he was in league with the devil—"

"You can hardly go by that," Phoebe said. "Tempesta is always saying things like that. She thinks *The Wizard of Oz* is full of secret infernal messages."

"I know," I said, "but that's the point. When I got that letter, what

really struck me was that for once I almost believed her. Damon Rask
is—"

"If you tell me he has horns and a tail, I'm going to get out and
walk."

"He doesn't have horns and a tail. He looks more normal than we
do. Nice suits. Narrow ties. Good shirts. Wing-tips. He could be, I
don't know, somebody's broker. The kind of broker that doesn't get
indicted."

"So?"

"So he's strange, Phoebe. He's really strange. Scary strange."

"It must be the air up here," Phoebe said. "You're not making any
sense at all."

We'd gotten to the curve in the drive. I swung us around, heading
for the garages and my Gold Coast relatives' collection of odd vehicles. It had started to snow again.

"I'm not going to tell you he did anything," I said, "because he
didn't. I'm not going to tell you he said anything, either, at least not
anything out of the ordinary. It's not anything I could describe so it
makes sense. But let me tell you something. I'd like to know what he
did with his life before he became a trance channeler."

"Isn't it in his author bio?"

"You can put anything you want in an author bio, Phoebe. Remember Tiffany Baxter."

We both remembered Tiffany Baxter. Her real name was Corinne
Patalevski, and she wrote historical romances about Tibet. For her
author bio, she'd invented not only her name, but a college, a graduate school, a house in Palm Beach and an entire island.

I cut the engine and looked out at Uncle Robert's tank. It wasn't
really a tank any more. He'd had the treads removed. The state of
Connecticut hadn't been happy with the idea of those treads on its
roads. He'd had the metal wheels replaced with oversized radials, too,
so the thing was a little like a military hot rod. The effect was just like
Robert's own: happy, confused, and completely irrational.

It occurred to me that everyone in my family was crazy, except my
mother. She was something else again.

Phoebe poked me in the ribs. "So?" she said.

"So what?"

"So what about Damon Rask?"

I put my cigarette out. "Look," I said, "I won't say he's the kind of person you wouldn't want to meet in a dark alley, because he's nothing like a thug. But I *wouldn't* want to meet him in a dark alley. He's—cold, I guess. You just get the feeling that he could do anything and not give a shit about it afterward."

"Stop swearing. That's your mother coming down the porch steps."

"Sorry. Remember when Myrra Agenworth died and we decided—well, we decided that the woman who killed her must be a psychopath? But she didn't come off like a psychopath. She just came off normal. Well, Damon Rask comes off like a psychopath. Or a sociopath. Or whatever we call them nowadays."

"Help me out of this seat belt."

I popped the lock for her. "You know I like murder mysteries," I said, "and you know I've never thought twice in my life when I've had a chance to get involved in one. But I wouldn't want to be involved in a tea party if Damon Rask was part of it."

"Then you'd better elope, Patience. You invited that Delia Grantham person to your wedding. I saw the list."

I stared at her, startled. She was right. Delia *had* been invited to the wedding. And where Delia went, her husband would undoubtedly follow.

I started to say something inane—like how I should have eloped to begin with—when I heard a heavy pounding at my side. I looked out my window to find my mother kicking at my door, her salt-and-pepper hair bouncing in the stiff wind. I pounded back until I got her attention and made shooing motions until she got far enough away from the Jeep to allow me to open up. Then I realized I'd completely forgotten about her all the time Phoebe and I had been talking about Damon Rask, and I was startled all over again. I'd always thought Armageddon wouldn't be enough to distract me from brooding about my mother.

Out on the drive, Mother started gesturing, moving her arms in great arcs, as if she were guiding an ocean liner into port.

"Christ," I said, "hardly even parked, and already she's at it."

"She's just glad to see you, Patience."

I gave Phoebe my best look ever, the kind I'd always wished I could visit on my mother. Then I shoved my pack of cigarettes into my jacket pocket and jumped out of the Jeep.

"I just got here," I said as I hit the ground. "Give me half a second to get myself together, will you please?"

Mother looked me up and down, back and forth, the way she always does when she hasn't seen me in a while—meaning for more than fifteen minutes. Then she said, "I don't have time to indulge your dallying, Patience. I need your help. I have a dead body in my living room, and it's already been there for *six hours.*"

FOUR

MY MOTHER is what Litchfield County likes to think of as Old School. She believes in Protestant rectitude and the invincibility of Christian morality, with "Christian" defined the way it was during the reign of Theodore Roosevelt. She takes care of herself without being excessive about it. She doesn't smoke and rarely drinks, but she's a good twenty pounds heavier than a New Yorker would want to be and she wouldn't allow an exercise tape in her house. In fact, she doesn't allow televisions. She's reached the ripe old age of seventy-one without having the faintest idea who Johnny Carson is.

She's also reached the ripe old age of seventy-one without ever having to compromise her principles—and that, I've found, is a hard thing to live with. My life is always a mess, full of confusion and violence, compromise and uncertainty. My mother's life is a newly graded road with a fresh cap of asphalt on top of it. It was self-delusion to say I'd moved to New York just to escape from Waverly, Connecticut. I'd moved to New York to escape from my mother—and from living up to my mother, which was worse.

I stood next to the Jeep and watched her walking back to the house, a small, sturdy woman in a Litchfield County uniform: flowered skirt, white shirt, oversized crew-neck sweater, espadrilles. Then I looked down at my cigarette and made a face. One of the things I'd promised her—in one of those three A.M. conversations about tea roses—was to at least try to quit smoking before the wedding.

"Patience," Phoebe said, from the other side of the car. "She only asked you to try. She isn't going to kill you because it didn't work out."

"Right," I said. My mother quit smoking in 1966. She'd been doing a pack a day for twenty years. She read the preliminary findings of the Surgeon General's report, decided it was a stupid thing to go on doing, threw all her cigarettes in the trash—and never looked back.

I threw my own cigarette on the drive, stomped on it until it was out, and then picked it up, so I wouldn't create litter. My mother hates litter.

"Just a minute," I told Phoebe. "I'll get you out in a minute."

"Get me out now," Phoebe said. "I thought I heard your mother say something about a dead body."

I said "mmm," and went around the back to release Phoebe from her bondage. On the way, I checked out Elizabeth's little black BMW two-door. People like Elizabeth always have little black BMW two-doors.

I got Phoebe's door open and held my arm out for her to lean on. "She did say something about a dead body. In the living room. For the past six hours."

"For heaven's sake," Phoebe said. "Why aren't we *hurrying?* Don't you want to know what it's all about?"

"No."

"Patience."

"Trust me," I said. "It'll have something to do with Felicia. Or dear old Aunt Cordie. Why a fifty-year-old woman would want to go on being called Cordie is beyond me. And if it isn't either of them, it's Elizabeth. Or Robert. Or even my father. And no matter which one of them it is—"

"You think your own father may be dead and you're standing out here *complaining* about it?"

"Phoebe," I said, "if Daddy were dead, Mother would have said so. All I meant was that I thought he might be responsible for the body."

"Responsible for the body how?"

"I haven't the faintest idea. We've never had a body out here before."

"Do you think it's a murder?"

I shook my head. "You've got murder on the brain," I said. "We haven't had a murder in Waverly for— well, forever. Unless Old Will Marsh was murdered, which I doubt. Maybe Uncle Robert picked up some dead tramp and now he wants to—"

"Patience."

"Here's the difference between you and me," I said. "You don't think they'd do something like that. I know they would."

She gave me a funny look I recognized. It was the look Nick always gave me whenever I talked about home. Then she shrugged her shoulders and headed off toward the house.

Sometimes I don't give my mother enough credit—maybe to balance the times when I give her too much. I'd been sure she was going to disappear, leaving me to face my Gold Coast relatives, and an unidentified dead body, unprepared. She had a host of very good reasons to do just that. They weren't *her* relatives. She was the only child of only children. It was my father who was one of eight, and his father who was one of fifteen. There were McKennas all over the landscape, but the Campbells were a dying race.

"Listen," my mother always said, whenever I complained about one or another of the nuts, "I only married them, Patience. They may be my cross, but they're certainly not my fault."

That day, she must have decided they were her responsibility—at least as far as I was concerned. She hadn't disappeared at all. She was waiting in the foyer when Phoebe and I came into the house, standing to the side of the half-opened living room door at an angle calculated to make her invisible to the people inside. She looked up when we came in and nodded a little.

"Take a look," she said. "Try not to let them see you. I'm not ready to go back to the fray."

I looked. Our living room is an immense space, thirty-five feet by sixty, taking up the entire length, and almost half the width, of the main part of the house. Usually, it is dominated by the oversized fieldstone fireplace at the center of the longest unbroken wall. The fireplace looks medieval-functional, even though it isn't. It always makes me think of whole pigs roasting on spits over open fires. There was a fire going in it today—as there always is, winter and summer— but it was hidden behind a magnificent rosewood casket. An *immense* magnificent rosewood casket. I'd never seen a casket that long. It must have been custom-made.

I looked back at my mother. "There's nobody in there," I said. "Except the—"

"Look again," Mother said.

I looked again. Eventually, I found them—huddled in a little knot of misery near the back windows. My father was the most miserable of them all. Most of the time, he's the most relaxed of all men, so fluid his bones seem to be made of mercury. Now he had rolled himself into a stiff, lumpy ball in the middle of a Campbell plaid wingbacked chair. Every once in a while, he turned his head to the right or to the left. Almost immediately, he decided he didn't like what he saw there, and went back to staring at his knees.

I didn't like what I saw there, either. To Daddy's left was my cousin Elizabeth, starchy-dour in a Villager skirt-and-sweater set and a pair of flat-heeled shoes. Elizabeth was the only person I knew who could still *find* Villager skirt-and-sweater sets—and add-a-pearl necklaces, button-downs without vest pockets and knee socks that matched her hair ribbons. We were only four months apart in age, but she could have stepped out of a Vassar recruiting brochure, circa 1962. She had not, however, gone to Vassar. Her grades were never good enough. She'd spent two years at Colby-Sawyer in New Hampshire, and come home expecting to be married in a week.

Unfortunately, Elizabeth was less like the thirties debutantes she admired than she was like her own mother, my long-dead Aunt Rosamund. Rosamund was a legend in the family, possibly the most tactless, awkward, unyielding harridan ever to bear the McKenna name. She drove Elizabeth's father to a heart attack at the age of forty-seven, and then herself to one three years later. Elizabeth was left to be raised by our Great-Aunt Felicia, and fed on stories of the lost glamour of being young and rich in 1922. The result was distinctly unpleasant. Elizabeth was not only a twit, she was a malicious little bitch—and she *liked* herself that way.

On the other side of my father sat my Aunt Cordie, the most bewildering person I had ever met. My brother George once said Cordie had been lobotomized at birth, and I half believed him. She was a profoundly stupid woman. Once the reigning star of a triumphant Farmington's field hockey team, she had advanced to the age of fifty *determined* never to lose her grip on what she called her "Identity." She wore her frequently dyed chestnut-brown hair cut short and pulled off her face by a pair of tortoiseshell combs. She stuffed her sagging body into balloon-hipped jodhpurs and polished riding boots. She promenaded through stables and houses with a crash-heeled Ge-stapo stomp that shook foundations and threatened china. She had no conversation that didn't relate to upper-class women's sports. She could read you chapter and verse on the latest round of junior horse shows. The last president she'd actually known the name of had been Eisenhower.

Like a lot of stupid people, once Cordie got an idea in her head, it was impossible to get it out again. She was in the grip of one of her ideas now. Her face was screwed up tight. She looked like the Pillsbury Doughboy would have if the Pillsbury Doughboy ever got a stomachache.

On the far side of Cordie sat my Uncle Robert, looking even more miserable than my father did. That, I thought, was fitting. Daddy and Robert were the only members of that generation who were really close, and the only ones who seemed to have anything besides money in common. They were tall, thin men with thinning hair and a taste for the ridiculous. Daddy took his out in Mickey Mouse watches and Godzilla cigarette lighters. Robert had more of a bent for the spectacular. There was that tank, and there were a few accessories to go with it. A hot tub that circulated pink champagne. An ice-cream machine that produced flavors like broccoli and pâté de foie gras. A set of pencils with "Jesus Loves You!" printed on the sides and the head of a cherub on a spring attached to the eraser ends. If Daddy was upset, Robert would be upset along with him.

On the other side of Robert sat my Great-Aunt Felicia, but I didn't pause speculating over her. There was nothing charmingly, or even annoyingly, whimsical about Felicia. She had that ramrod-straight spine women of her generation were forced to adopt by Parisian finishing schools, and a habit of mind that had a great deal in common with Clausewitz. Or maybe Bismarck. Somehow, although she didn't go in for costumes and had a positive horror of anachronisms—no cane for Great-Aunt Felicia, and no lacy white blouses, either—she always reminded me of Queen Elizabeth I on the day she ordered the execution of Essex.

Felicia would have done that if she could: ordered the death of somebody. She would have started with me.

I turned back to Mother again. "They're not saying anything," I said.

Mother made a wry face. "Well, they have to shut up sometimes, don't they? If they yap without ceasing, they'll get laryngitis, and then they'll have to shut up altogether. And we could never have *that.*"

"But whose body is it?" Phoebe said. "Who's lying in the casket?"

"It isn't Aunt Eugenie, is it?" I asked.

"Your Aunt Eugenie is in the Bahamas," Mother said. "She'll be back for your wedding. And I must say, it's par for the course around here. The *one* member of that family with an ounce of common sense, and she's incommunicado in a villa when I need her. The person in the casket is your Great-Uncle Ephram Aurelius. He died the night before last."

"Oh," I said.

"But what's he doing *here?*" Phoebe said.

Mother sighed. "He used to live down in Greenwich near Robert, and when he died Robert brought him up here, because naturally Robert thought—"

"Robert brought him up here in the tank?" I said.

"Of course not," Mother said. "Robert called George and George took the train down and Robert had a rented hearse all ready. What did you think?"

"Excuse me," I said.

"Anyway," Mother said, "they got up here this morning, and naturally they thought they were going to bury him in family cemetery, that's what the family cemetery's for, after all, but—"

"I didn't know people had family cemeteries," Phoebe said. "Anymore, I mean."

"People don't have family cemeteries anymore," Mother said. "They've been outlawed in the state of Connecticut. But it's like everything else. There's a grandfather clause in that law, and like always, the McKennas got the benefit of it."

"What's a grandfather clause?" Phoebe said.

"When they outlaw something that used to be allowed," I told her, "they always make a provision that lets the people who are still doing it go on doing it, and just makes it illegal for anybody to start doing it. If you see what I mean."

"I see what you mean," Phoebe said.

"The McKenna family cemetery has been in operation since 1689," Mother said, "and it's huge. It's going to be in operation for years to come. God only knows what they were thinking of way back then. I mean, I know it was the custom to have large families, and I know the McKennas had larger families than most, but still. Ten solid acres."

"Ten solid acres?" Phoebe looked as if she thought my mother had flipped.

"The cemetery is the wedge," I said helpfully. "Remember when we were talking about the Deverton place? Well, even if you could talk the zoning board into letting you develop it, you couldn't develop it. Our cemetery makes a big arrow-shaped intrusion into the property."

"Develop the Deverton place." Mother shuddered.

Phoebe looked confused. "But I don't understand," she said. "Everything's all right, isn't it? Here's Great-Uncle Whoever—"

"Ephram Aurelius," Mother said.

"—and here's the cemetery, with lots of room in it—"

"Lots," Mother agreed.

"And now all you have to do is hold a funeral and bury him."

"You would think so," Mother said, "wouldn't you?"

"Am I missing something?" Phoebe said.

Mother raised her eyebrows at me, and I nodded. Phoebe was indeed missing something—but it wasn't something she could be expected to know. I leaned back and took another look at the crowd in the living room. As far as I could tell, none of them had moved.

"Cordie looks about ready to wet her pants," I said. "What caused the impasse?"

"Felicia," Mother said.

"Naturally," I said.

Mother turned to Phoebe. "Burial in the McKenna family cemetery," she explained, "is restricted to direct descendants of John George McKenna and their spouses. John George McKenna was a very liberal man for his time. When we have somebody who qualifies, we call the funeral parlor and they do what they have to do to comply with state burial regulations. At least, that's what we usually do. The McKennas didn't get grandfathered out of *that.*"

"We just got stuck with the bill," I said. *"Have* you called the funeral parlor yet?"

"No," Mother said.

"You could always present her with a fait accompli," I pointed out.

"Would you want to? She'd probably insist on having the body dug up. And I don't know *what* I would do about that."

"Neither do I," I admitted.

"I was hoping you'd go in there and talk a lot of legal rigmarole and scare her to death," Mother said, "or get Nick up here and let *him* scare her to death. I don't know if it's possible, but it has to be worth a try."

I went back to the living room door again. The crowd still hadn't moved, and they still weren't talking. Daddy. Robert. Elizabeth. Cordie. Felicia. In the gloom made by dim lighting and a gray day, they looked like frozen leprechauns on a death watch.

Felicia shifted in her chair, her stiff joints and brittle bones working laboriously to produce something like grace. I could almost hear her creak.

"Go," Mother said, pushing at the small of my back.

I went, but not fast enough. Felicia caught me just before I came stumbling into the room. From the look on her face, I knew she thought I was trying to sneak up on her.

She turned all the way around, to face me, and raised her arm—in either a salute or a command to stop. Then she said,

"Don't even bother to try, Patience. Ephram Aurelius McKenna was no McKenna at all. He was adopted out of the Hendershot family at the age of six, and I won't have him poisoning my eternity the way he poisoned my life."

FIVE

IT WAS MY PERSONAL OPINION that Felicia had poisoned all the lives she'd ever come in contact with—but Felicia wasn't the kind of woman you argued with, and Mother was expecting me to do something. I edged further into the living room, trying not to look at what I could feel: Phoebe, sneaking in behind me. It was one of the oddities of Phoebe's relationship with my mother that, although she had met all my relatives, she hadn't seen *me* with any of them. She just kept running into them on her visits to the house. Now, obviously, she wanted to see how I behaved when surrounded. It was more interesting than a dead body with no place to go.

Once I got into the living room proper, it seemed less gloomy than funereal—which was appropriate. I gave my Gold Coast relatives a closer look than I'd been able to from the foyer. With less distance, and less atmosphere, to cloud the issue, most of them showed signs of having had a long, hard day. Cordie's riding boots were covered with mud. The hem of Elizabeth's skirt was soggy and beginning to pucker. Even Robert, who had a positive mania for looking like something out of a Cary Grant movie, was rumpled. I remembered Susanna telling me they'd all been in to the Chestnut Tree this morning, and wondered what else they'd been doing. Why they'd been doing it was no problem at all. They'd wanted to get away from Felicia.

Now, with the monumental lack of practical imagination characteristic of all the McKennas, they had run out of excuses for escape. They were not only angry, but stuck. They fidgeted. They puckered. They stared at me in resentment. They did not move. They were a single mind with a single thought. Whoever moved first was going to get killed.

I made a halfhearted stab at rousing my father to action, but it didn't work. I got a smile of sympathy and an almost undetectable shrug. With no way out, I decided to take Bold and Decisive Action— something I am not good at, and have never been able to get away

with. Whatever. I marched over to the casket, keeping Felicia in sight
at all times, and looked down at Uncle Ephram Aurelius Hendershot
McKenna.

Oddly enough, considering all the dead bodies I've been exposed to
since the death of Myrra Agenworth changed my life, I'd never seen a
corpse prepped for burial before. When I'd attended funerals where
the coffin was open for "viewing," I'd found ways of staying out of
view. One look at Ephram Aurelius, and I decided I'd been right.
Undertakers really did make bodies look like wax. Ephram Aurelius
looked like a wax apple. His cheeks were much too red. His lips
would have done credit to a vampire. Even his tie was scarlet. His suit
was too tight.

"He looks a hundred and six," I said to no one in particular.

Robert piped up, "He was ninety-four. Does that suit look really
awful? It's one of mine, you see, and Ephram was a much bigger
man—"

"Everything Ephram wore always looked awful," Elizabeth said. "I
don't see why that should change *now.*"

Robert blushed as red as Ephram's tie—and his own. "He wouldn't
have looked so awful if anybody ever paid attention to him," he said.
"None of you ever liked him. That's the truth."

"None of us ever saw him," my father said.

"I saw him," Elizabeth said. "He was always hanging around the
house."

"He was a poor, confused old man and you people treated him like
sludge," Robert said. Then he glared at all of them, even Felicia. For
once, the glares he got back did nothing to make him back down.

I wandered the rest of the way across the living room to them,
getting my cigarettes out as I walked. Felicia hated smoking—they all
did; they had that upper-class horror of cigarettes that says that only
really tacky people like tobacco—but I was in no mood to accommo-
date Felicia at the moment. Especially since I knew Felicia didn't mind
smoking at all when she went to France. If she had, she'd have had to
sever her relations with half the House of Bourbon—and the House
of Bourbon was Felicia's spiritual home.

I put a cigarette in my mouth, lit up, blew a stream of smoke at the
ceiling, and sat down on the arm of my father's chair. "Now," I said,
"as far as I can tell, that's an embalmed body in that casket—"

"Oh, it's definitely embalmed," Robert said. "I had that done before we came up here."

"Fine. I don't know how long it takes an embalmed body to begin to—uh—deteriorate, but in my experience funerals are held *fairly* soon after deaths, so it just might make sense—just *might,* mind you— to do something about this one before we have a problem."

Felicia twitched. "I'm not objecting to *doing* something about the body, Patience. I'm merely objecting to burying it in the McKenna family cemetery. I would be more than happy to see it put in the ground someplace else."

"Where?" Robert said. "Potter's Field?"

"Put it any place you want to, Robert. Put it in your cellar, for all I care."

"He died in my cellar," Robert said. "My God, what an awful thing."

Elizabeth stirred in her chair. "He was an awful thing," she said. "He'd come sneaking around the house, pulling everything out of the trash cans—"

"There was a McKenna who had to go scrounging around in ash cans?" I was surprised.

"I think he had Alzheimer's disease," Robert said sadly. "I invited him to live with me, more than once. And he'd come, too. But he'd never stay long. I'd have him a week or ten days and he'd disappear, and then I'd find him down at one of the shelters or sleeping in one of the parks someplace. He kept—forgetting who he was, I guess."

"He was a horrid old man," Elizabeth said. "And he stank."

Robert stood up. "Of course he *stank,"* he said. "He never knew what day it was. He never knew how long it had been since he'd had a bath. Or a meal. Or a bed to sleep in. He was sick, for God's sake. What's wrong with you, Elizabeth? He was a sick old man and you—"

"He was a common variety *tramp,"* Elizabeth said. "That was all he was. He'd probably been drinking himself into a stupor for years—"

"—never drank a day in his life—"

"—and I don't see how we could have expected anything else. Blood will tell."

"Oh, for God's sake," I said. "I'm with Robert, Elizabeth. What the hell's wrong with you? You sound like a Victorian melodrama."

Elizabeth glared at my cigarette, glared at Robert, glared at me. "Ask Robert how Ephram died in his cellar. Just *ask* him."

I turned to Robert. Robert shrugged. "He had a heart attack," he said.

Elizabeth threw up her hands. "He had a heart attack! He had a heart attack! I'm not talking about his goddamned heart attack. I'm talking about his breaking into your house—"

"He didn't have to break into my house," Robert said. "He had a key."

"But he didn't use his key," Elizabeth said triumphantly. "He was a natural thief. He broke your cellar window and went crawling through it in the middle of the night, and then he went scrounging around through all your things and ate up all your strawberry preserves, and then he—"

"And then he died, Elizabeth."

"He was a natural thief," Elizabeth said again. "I'm with Great-Aunt Felicia on this one. I don't want him lying in the same ground with *me.*"

"Does anybody?" I asked.

They all turned to me. Whatever they had been expecting me to do, it wasn't this. I had them confused for the moment. I thought I'd better use that advantage for as long as I had it. I turned to Robert and gave him an encouraging look.

"Of course I want him buried here," Robert said. "That's why I brought him here."

"I want him buried here, too," my father said. "Ephram was all right, Patience. Not too bright and not too steady these last few years, but all right." He thought about it. "Your brother agrees with me, too," he said finally. "George said—" He threw a sudden, frightened look at Great-Aunt Felicia and shut up.

I smiled. "I can just *imagine* what George said."

"So can I," my mother said, "except I don't have to, because I heard it. And before you ask, I'm for burying Ephram here, too. I quite honestly can't see why not."

"Of course you can't," Elizabeth said. "You're not a McKenna, are you?"

"No," Mother said pleasantly, "I'm not. God has been very good to me."

"All right," I said. "Mother, Daddy, Robert, George and me for burying him here—"

"I don't think Aunt Louisa should be allowed to vote, Patience," Elizabeth said.

I ignored her. "—Elizabeth and Felicia for doing something else with him," I finished. "What about Cordie?"

We all looked at Cordie. She'd been so quiet during the conversation, we'd almost forgotten about her. I had blanked her right out. Now it occurred to me that that was very strange. Cordie was not a quiet woman. She wasn't a prudent one, either. Most of the time, she thought nothing of jumping feet first into the worst kind of holocaust.

At the moment, she wasn't jumping anywhere, feet or anything else first. She was just sitting in her chair, her arms wrapped around her chest, looking beatific and a little glazed. And she was smiling—a happy, idiot-child smile that made me distinctly uneasy.

"Cordie?" I said.

"Agahn egahn *hahn,*" Cordie said.

"What?" I said.

"Oh *no,*" Elizabeth said.

Cordie began to rock in her chair, her smile getting wider and wider and wider. "Agahn egahn *hahn,*" she said again, and then, "dulcilet dinvero capumer casca casca *coe.* Casca *coe coe coe!*"

"Patience." It was Phoebe, coming up behind me, whispering directly in my ear. "I don't know—"

Elizabeth jumped out of her chair. "Oh *you,*" she said, as if she'd just discovered Phoebe, for the first time in her life. *"You* don't *know.* Well *I* know. And I can't *take* it any more. I just can't *take* it."

"Can't take what?" I demanded. "What's going on here? What's she doing?"

"She isn't *doing,*" Felicia said drily. "She's *being.* As far as I've been able to understand it, *what* she's being is an Algonquin Indian princess who died on her property in Greenwich in the year 332."

"Felicia, for God's sake," I said. "The Algonquins didn't live in Greenwich. I don't think anybody lived in Greenwich in 332."

"That's all right," Felicia said. "Whenever she gets anything wrong, she just tells you it's because her mind's been scrambled. Because of all the times she was kidnapped by aliens, you know."

"Coe coe *coe,*" Cordie said.

"For God's *sake,*" I said again.

But it was really too late for God or anyone else—unless we were to be treated to a full scale miracle, which we weren't. Cordie was out of her chair, doing what I could only describe as dancing. She had her hands in the air over her head. She had her hips moving in a slither-and-jerk that was almost epileptic. The glaze in her eyes was now total. Looking into them, I could almost believe she was as dead as Ephram Aurelius.

I hadn't taken it seriously before, but now I had to. Cordie snaked her way down the length of the living room and began to circle the casket. Her combs were coming out of her hair. Her riding stock was becoming untied. Her belt had slipped the tongue of its buckle and begun to unwind under her sweater. She brought her hands down across her chest and grabbed her breasts so hard, it made me wince.

"Casca casca coe coe coe," she said.

I looked around frantically for my mother, only to find her standing at my elbow, practically breathing down my neck. "Is she all right?" I asked. "How long do these things go on?"

"I don't know," Mother said. "I've only heard about them. I've never seen one before. And I heard from Elizabeth and Felicia, so I don't know what to believe."

"What did they say?"

"That Cordie got religion and has been going into trances ever since. At parties, apparently."

"At parties?"

"Elizabeth said she pulled one of these at the Metropolitan's Spring Benefit Ball."

I turned my attention back to Cordie. She had let go of her breasts —thank God; even looking at that had been painful—and was concentrating on rubbing her palms against the wood of the casket. She rubbed and rubbed and rubbed, first the lid, then the sides, back and forth and up and down, until she came to a stop next to Ephram's head. She raised her hands in the air again and said,

"Kemma dorman. Kemma dorman. Ageth nolgru doh."

"Patience." Phoebe plucked at my sleeve. "I think you'd better stop this. I think you'd better stop this right now, because I think she's going to—"

She was going to, but none of us stopped her, because none of us could move. Cordie leaned over the casket, opened her mouth, and sucked Ephram's lips in. It was the worst sound I'd ever heard. It was wet and choked, and there was a tinge of the sexual to it that made my stomach turn.

"Dear God," I said.

"I'm going to be ill," my mother said. "For the first time in my life, Patience, I'm going to be ill."

"I'll get her," I said.

But I didn't have time to get her. I had just started to move forward when she stopped, jerking back as if she'd been lassoed around the neck.

"Kemma *creck,*" she said. "Kemma *creck.*"

She gripped the side of the casket and her body began to buck and jerk, buck and jerk, erupting in rhythmic spasms so violent they began to shake the coffin on its frame. The damn thing must have weighed a ton. Ephram Aurelius had been an exceptionally tall man, even if he had been thin, and the casket itself was the heavy, expensive kind. It had enough metal on it to have provided munitions for the Colonial army.

"Kemma creck," Cordie shouted. "Kemma creck kemma creck kemma creck."

She threw her hands into the air and brought them down again, smashing against the wood. The casket rocked, seesawed, settled in again.

"Galganda *foh,*" Cordie screamed, and pushed at the casket again, ramming her fists into it. This time it reared up to one side and did a little jump, and Elizabeth started screaming.

"Oh my God oh my God oh my God why doesn't somebody do something?"

"Agahn ameda akka acara reh," Cordie wailed. Then she ran back, halfway across the room, whirled in place, and threw out her arms.

"Now," Mother said.

I went at her, the only person in the room both young enough and big enough to have a chance at stopping her. She was spinning in place, pistoning her arms, pumping her knees up halfway to her chin. I didn't think I had a chance in hell of grabbing her in the ordinary way. I braced myself against my mother's best buhl writing table and launched. I was half a second too late.

I saw the heels of her riding boots just above my hands as I hit the floor. When I looked up, she was charging across the room again, her arms held out rigidly in front of her, charging at that casket as if it were as soft and welcoming as a stripper's stageside curtain. She slammed into it at top speed. This time it didn't even bother to rock. It just slid.

"*Evoe,*" Cordie screamed.

The casket fell forward, catching on the rim of the frame. The jerking half-stop dislodged the body. Ephram Aurelius came tumbling onto the living room floor, his weight and sudden movement splitting the seams of Uncle Robert's suit.

"*EVOE,*" Cordie screamed again.

This time, I was just close enough. I got my hand around her ankle just before she tried to throw herself on Ephram's body, and I brought her down.

She hit the floor with the force of a seismic eruption, and the last thing she said was,

"Evoe!"

The last thing anyone else said came from my Great-Aunt Felicia.

"If you think this nonsense is going to change my mind about the cemetery," she said, "you're wrong."

SIX

I DON'T KNOW what would have happened then if nothing had happened then. Mother had been threatening to "do something" to Felicia for years. It was the only sign of temper I'd ever seen in her. Now she turned to my great-aunt the way she turned on the snakes she found in her garden, and I thought an explosion was inevitable. The situation was such an unholy mess. Cordie was on the floor. Ephram Aurelius's body was on the floor. The casket was standing on its top end and rocking. Any minute now it was going to fall over.

It did fall over. Elizabeth, with the distracted frenzy of an essentially lazy person who has finally decided to take action, leaped to her feet, apparently intent on keeping Mother and Felicia apart. When she hit the floorboards, they shuddered. The tremor passed under the casket at the worst possible moment. The casket did another little hop in the air, spun halfway around, and crashed into the fireplace screen.

In fact, it crashed through the fireplace screen, and it was heavy enough to make shreds of three layers of fireproofed wire. An arc of sparks and glowing wood chips flew into the room, scattering all over my grandmother Mary Louisa Campbell's blue-and-gold Persian rug. Mother spun away from Felicia—I think she'd been meaning to strangle her—and grabbed her best embroidered tea cloth from the surface of the coffee table.

"Water," Mother said. "I've got to have water on some of these. There's going to be a fire."

"I'll get water," Phoebe said, taking the cloth out of Mother's hand. She headed for the kitchen, and I called after her, "Don't get water on that thing. Use the terrycloth dish towels."

"Patience, for God's sake, do something," Mother said. "Do something now."

Grandmother Mary Louisa Campbell's rug was very old. It had worn spots in all the right places, a quality highly prized in Persian rugs in old-money enclaves like Waverly. Unfortunately, worn spots catch faster than ordinary rug nap does. Little puffs of smoke had begun to rise from every one of them. Little puffs of smoke had begun to rise from Cordie's jodhpurs, too.

I put Cordie out first. It wasn't difficult, since she'd only begun to smolder. "Grab her feet," I told Mother. "We'll get everything off the rug and fold it up." Then I turned on Elizabeth. "Will you get off your butt?" I demanded. "Do you intend to sit there while the house burns down?"

"I'm not going to touch *that man,* Patience. I'd rather go up in flames like Joan of Arc."

"Joan of Arc was a saint, Elizabeth. At the moment, I don't think you could make it through the gates of Purgatory."

"I've got Cordie off," Mother said. "I need help with Ephram Aurelius."

I turned my back on Elizabeth, and was gratified to find that Daddy and Robert had joined the rescue mission. They were trying to lift the dead old man and finding it impossible. Daddy and Robert are both slight men, weak, really. Neither one of them had ever gone in for bodybuilding, and neither one of them had ever had much of a body to build up. Ephram Aurelius had had, once. Much of it was now wasted away, but he was still bulky enough, and heavy-boned enough, to be a problem for the Dynamic Duo. I rushed over to them, shooed them back, and said,

"Roll."

They rolled. I grabbed one end of the casket and shoved, moving it about half an inch. The idiotic thing was unbelievably heavy, as if it had been weighted to sink at sea. Mother got hold of the other end and started to drag. With both of us working, we managed to get the casket moving.

"Off," Daddy called to us from the other side of the room, meaning Ephram Aurelius was finally clear of the rug.

Something switched on inside my mother's head. Instead of thanking him, she began to shout—and I'd never heard her shout before in my life.

"John," she said, "this is *it.* Do you hear me? This is *it.* I have had these people in my house for the last time. The very last time, John. I will not—"

"Now, Louisa," Daddy said.

"Don't you *dare* 'now Louisa' me. I have been insulted. I have been invaded. I have been nagged, tortured, and driven halfway out of my mind. I will not be burned to a crisp."

"They're our *family,* Louisa."

We had the casket all the way to the edge of the rug closest to the foyer door. Mother jerked her end of it hard and got a good third of it onto bare wood. I pushed my end and didn't do so well. Behind us, the smoldering was beginning to turn into something worse, and the smoke was getting thick. My eyes were stinging. Elizabeth's eyes must have been stinging, too. She had edged her way around the room and was on her way to the foyer.

I gave the casket another shove. Mother gave it another pull. It snagged, caught, resisted and, unexpectedly, popped free. Then it slid, scraped, screeched, and settled with a groan on Mother's two-hundred-year-old wideboard floor.

"There," I said, feeling a little confused.

Phoebe came rushing in from the kitchen, her arms full of sopping wet terrycloth towels. "I've got the water," she said, breathless. "Where do I put it?"

Mother and I both turned to stare at her. It had gotten suddenly quiet—or it had been quiet all along, and we hadn't been aware of it. Elizabeth hadn't quite made it out of the room. She was flattened against the wall between the living room and the foyer, with her hair against the frame of the portrait of my great-great-grandfather Thomas and her hands flat on the faded old rose of a silk wall hanging. Daddy and Robert were out of sight, probably back there where it had all started, keeping out of Mother's way. None of us had heard from Felicia in what felt like forever.

And it wasn't long enough.

Mother and I swung all the way around, at once, to check out the far end of the room. Daddy and Robert were indeed there, and so was Felicia—but Daddy and Robert were behaving like normal people. They looked exhausted and scared to death. Felicia was still in her chair. Her brow was clear. Her hands were still. Her feet were planted firmly on the floor. She even had a little smile on her face. She hadn't moved a millimeter.

"Dear sweet Lord," Mother said, under her breath. "That *woman.*"

There was a little lick of flame starting up in the very center of the rug. I took one of Phoebe's sopping towels and walked over to it. I dropped the towel to the floor, ground it under my foot, and said, "I

think we'd better get this thing rolled up. We can throw it out the
front door."

"Yes, yes," Mother said. "The front door. We can throw it in the
snow."

"Are you two all right?" Phoebe said.

"Of course they're not all right," Felicia said—and she sounded like
she always did, really, except that her voice was a little raspy, the way
people's voices get when they've been scraped by smoke. "Of course
they're not all right," she said again. "They've been panicking. Panicking always upsets the stomach."

At that moment, I think my mother would have killed her, bare-
handed and in an ecstasy of self-righteous justification. She was
stopped by the sound of the front door crashing open, and the clomp
of hobnailed boots on the foyer floor, and my brother George's voice
saying,

"What the hell is going on around here?"

My brother George is the only rich person I have ever known who has
been able to escape completely from his upbringing—or as completely
as he's wanted to, which comes to the same thing. Even after a decade
in New York, I am easily recognizable for what I am: the product of
dancing classes, boarding schools, and the lusher Connecticut countryside. George has managed to obliterate all that. He still has the uncon-
scious self-confidence of someone who has never had to worry about
money, but it's a self-confidence shared by the landed poor. They, too,
have never had to worry about money. It was as one of them that
George had decided to live out his life. He'd spent four years at
Groton and another two at the Massachusetts Institute of Technology,
but if he'd ever had a Groton accent or that MIT arrogance, there was
no trace of it now. He had a great deal of land, but so did the Carrs,
and the Carrs had been scraping along on welfare since FDR was
president. He had a big house, but so did Freddie Hanks, and Freddie
had made whatever money he had pumping gas on the Matheson
Road. Significantly, George's house was not old. He had built it himself. It was all cedar and glass and outsized decks. If you wanted to be
nasty about it—and Elizabeth often did—you could call it the world's
ultimate raised ranch.

Most rich people who wear poor people's clothes look fake in them.
George looked like he'd been born in shitkickers and Lee Riders. The

very sight of him drove Elizabeth crazy and turned Felicia white.
Cordie always said it was all Kathy's fault, as if she hadn't noticed that
George had changed years before he met Kathy, and wouldn't have
met Kathy if he hadn't changed.

He came into the living room, checked out the Gold Coast relatives, checked out our parents, then checked out the smoldering rug.
Ephram Aurelius's body was practically under his feet. He must have
noticed it. He didn't even blink.

"That thing's on fire," he said—as if, of all the people he knew, I
was the one who was supposed to make sense.

"I know," I said.

"You know." He kicked at it. "Don't you think we ought to get it
out of here before something else catches?"

"Believe it or not," I said, "we've been trying to."

"I came over to give you a note from your friend Delia the jerk.
She's having some kind of party."

He stepped over Ephram's body, picked up the rug by one end, and
flipped it into a fold. "Give me a second. I've got to put this in the
yard."

"On the *lawn,*" Great-Aunt Felicia said.

George ignored her, and the rest of us ignored her, too. George
dropped the mail on Mother's buhl writing table, folded the rug in
half again and then again, and hefted it onto his shoulders. It smelled
awful, dry and harsh.

"Heavy," he said, to no one in particular. And to me: "Your friend
Delia really is a jerk. She trills when she talks. And if you think you're
talking me into going to that thing, you're nuts."

He marched through the living room, through the foyer, and out
the front door. We all heard his steps on the porch and the thud as the
rug hit the snow.

"I don't know where he gets it," Elizabeth said. "You'd think he'd
been raised by a maid."

I was about to tell her I thought she'd been raised by Dracula's
daughters, but I could hear George again. George's boots are so
heavy, you can hear him coming over any kind of surface, no matter
how soft. I kept my mouth shut and waited for him to get back into the
room. Now that he was here, not even my mother felt any great need
to do anything. We were all too used to letting George do it for us.

"So," he said, when he finally reappeared among us. "What did go on here, anyway?"

"Cordie had one of her—fits," Mother said.

"Oh." George looked down at Ephram Aurelius, nodded a little, and stepped over his body once again. "We'd better get this thing set up again," he said, patting the casket. "Come over here and lever it for me, Pay."

I went over. I put my hand under one end. George did the rest of the work. In no time at all, the casket was back on its frame, looking battered but basically stable. George went back to Ephram Aurelius, picked him up, and carried him back into position. Then he dumped him back into the casket.

"Somebody else is going to have to rearrange him," he said. "I wouldn't begin to know how."

"I'll rearrange him," Mother said.

"Did you have to just throw him like that?" Elizabeth said. "Don't you have any respect for the dead?"

"No," Phoebe said, grabbing me by the arm. "Patience, don't."

I hadn't actually been going to, although it wasn't a bad idea. I was tired out, emotionally, physically, intellectually, and every other way. I couldn't have worked up the energy to take a good hard swallow. I watched George walk over to Cordie, and sent up a prayer of heartfelt thanksgiving that I wasn't going to have to find a way to get her up to bed.

"I think she's all right," I said. "I mean, I don't think she's dead."

"No, she's not dead." George shook his head. "But you guys ought to know by now, when she gets into one of those things, you've got to lock her up. She's not responsible."

"How was I supposed to know that? I never even knew she had—those things."

"*They* knew." George jerked his head back in the direction of Felicia. Elizabeth was still by the door. "Oh, never mind. You got some of those ampule things around anywhere? Maybe we can bring her out of it."

"I've got some in the bathroom upstairs," Mother said.

"It isn't going to do any good," Elizabeth said. "She'll sleep like that for hours."

George made an exasperated snort. "You're an even bigger jerk than Delia Grantham," he said. "We'll *try* to bring her out of it be-

cause I don't *want* to go carrying her all over this house on my goddamned *back,* do you get what I mean?"

"You always swear," Elizabeth said. "Have you ever noticed that?
You *always* swear."

"When I swear, I do a much better job than this."

"I'll go get the ammonia," Mother said. "Please. Don't fight."

She went running out of the room. We all turned our attention to
Cordie. George had rolled her over on her back and was checking her
head for bumps. He apparently found none. He would have an-
nounced it if he had.

"I hate having that idiot living right next door to me," he said,
giving us no chance to switch gears. "It's bad enough to have the
Deverton place, and the goddamned cemetery, but *this* jerk. You see
that house yet, Pay?"

"Oh," I said, "Damon Rask's house." I was very proud of myself.
When George switches subjects, it can take a mind the caliber of
Einstein's to figure out where the conversation's gone. "No," I said.
"I've heard he needed a lot of variances—"

"He needed his head examined," George said. "Damn thing looks
like a flying saucer. In midflight. It's been *reported* as a flying saucer
more than once. People see that glass dome with the moon shining on
it and think the Martians have landed."

"From what I know about Damon Rask, maybe the Martians *have*
landed," I said.

"If anybody's a Martian, it's that wife of his. That friend of yours.
Do you know what she's got up there? A garden full of poison
plants."

"Poison plants?" Phoebe said.

"Henbane," George said. "Mistletoe. Yew and oleander, for God's
sake. I think she worships them."

"Don't be ridiculous," Phoebe said. "Nobody worships plants."

Mother came hurrying back into the room, her fists full of cloudy
little ampules, the modern version of smelling salts.

"Here we are," she said. "Give these a try, George. If they don't
work, we'll have to call in the doctor."

George took the ampules out of Mother's hand, put all but one on
the floor beside Cordie's head, and broke the last one under her nose.
Nothing happened.

"Shit," he said.

"Now, George," Mother said.

"Cordie wouldn't *approve* of having a doctor in," Elizabeth said. "You ought to go upstairs and get her silly little crystal."

George broke another ampule under Cordie's nose instead. This time, she stirred and moaned and shivered. We all took it to be a very good sign.

"Give her another one," Mother urged George. "One more and I think we'll be getting somewhere."

"Silly little bitch," Felicia said.

George and Phoebe and Mother and Elizabeth and I all turned our heads in the direction of Felicia's voice, more out of surprise than anything else. She'd been quiet for so long, and we'd been so intent on the rug and Ephram and Cordie, we'd almost forgotten her. She had a talent for that, when she wanted to.

It was Elizabeth who noticed the difference first. Felicia was still sitting in her chair. She still had her feet flat on the floor and her hands on the armrests. At first glance, she looked the way she had all morning. It took determined staring in the dark to see the things that were wrong.

The blue cast to the skin. The unnatural cording of the muscles of the neck. That sudden clawlike rigidity of the hands. Elizabeth started across the room, looking frantic.

"Aunt Felicia? Aunt Felicia, what—"

But there was no question of *what*. Felicia grabbed for her chest, got a handful of blouse in her hand, and ripped. Strips of silk crepe de chine fell into her lap.

Then Felicia arched her back, grabbed at the arms of her chair once again, and died.

Cordie, of course, chose that moment to wake up. She pulled herself into a sitting position, blinked a vague gaze into all corners of the room, and stopped at the sight of Felicia, collapsed.

"Oh," Cordie said. "Felicia's dead, isn't she? Isn't that *nice.*"

SEVEN

NICK CARRAS sometimes says of me that I want every death to be a murder. Give me an ordinary cardiac arrest, and I will natter away at it for days, trying to turn it into a poisoning. This isn't entirely true. God only knows I'd just as soon all violence came to an abrupt stop, tomorrow, even on television. My adopted daughter is eight years old, and she's had enough blood in her life already. On the other hand, I have been around enough murders to be suspicious of any *convenient* death —and Felicia's death was certainly convenient. I couldn't imagine killing anyone just because she didn't want to be buried in the same cemetery as a poor old man, but most of the motives I've run into have seemed impossibly flimsy to me. Maybe I'm just not much of an obsessive.

If that was all there was to worry about, I probably wouldn't have worried. Felicia was an old woman, and, as George pointed out, she had both a history of heart trouble and a disinclination to do anything about it. I had known neither of those things, but everybody else seemed to. I took their word for it. Elizabeth kept wandering from the living room into the back hall and back into the living room again, blithering about how Felicia *never* took her pills and *never* watched her diet and *never* got any exercise.

What I was worried about was the way Felicia had looked while she was dying. I have seen someone die of poison—Adrienne's mother, in fact. I once almost died of it myself. I knew Felicia couldn't have died of arsenic. She'd had no vomiting, and her death had been far too clean. On the other hand, her death had been far too *weird* to be a simple heart attack.

Or I thought it had. That nobody else was going to think so was obvious without my ever broaching the subject, so I decided not to. I went out onto the porch instead. I got out my cigarettes—the rule about *never smoking at a crime scene* has been bludgeoned into my head, to the point where I can no longer smoke at funerals—and sat down in one of the gliders lined up against the wall. By then, the sky had turned black and the weather had turned nasty. Great glob-like snow-flakes were falling from the sky, threatening to turn into sleet. I lit up and leaned back, rocking a little on the glider's springs. That blue cast to the skin. Those clawlike hands. I almost wished I'd seen someone having a heart attack, just so I could make the comparison. Nothing I'd read had said anything about *claws*. And as for that blue cast—

I heard the front door open and looked up, expecting to see Phoebe. I saw George. He had shed his jacket inside, and I saw he was wearing one of the sweaters my mother buys him every Christmas at Brooks Brothers, instead of his usual plaid flannel shirt. The sweater was black cashmere and had a little block of embroidered initials just under the seam on the right shoulder: GXCM. George Xenophon Campbell McKenna. Our father has never recovered from the fact that they made him study ancient Greek in prep school.

George got one of the summer chairs from the stack on the other side of the door and sat down in it.

"I thought you were going to be Phoebe," I said. "I keep expecting her to whip out her magnifying glass and start peering into all the corners."

"Phoebe's helping Ma with Cordie," George said. *"She's* not having a nervous breakdown."

I made a face at him, and he laughed. George's English has gotten less and less precise over the years, but I had no trouble following his cavalier use of pronouns to its logical conclusion. Phoebe was the one who *wasn't* having the nervous breakdown. I was the one who *was*.

I jerked my head toward the front door and said, "I heard Mother calling somebody named Chris Bennett. Is that my Chris Bennett? Did my Chris Bennett become a *doctor?"*

"I don't want to talk about Chris Bennett," George said.

I made another face at him. My cigarette was burned almost to the filter, so I ground it out under my heel and tossed the butt far off into the snow. Then I lit another one. I almost never chain-smoke, but the urge to do it then was undeniable. I saw George's raised eyebrows and shrugged.

"I'm nervous," I said. "What do you expect?"

"A little common sense?" George said.

"If you mean about Felicia's dying, I am using common sense. I'm not running around the living room declaring she was murdered. I'm not even having a private little word with Mother. I'm just sitting out here smoking myself to death."

"Mother's got enough trouble without you getting Tommy Dick all worked up," George said. "And Tommy takes nothing to get worked up, these days. Tommy's been seeing ax murderers in the bushes for months."

"Which is supposed to mean what?"

"Which is supposed to mean he's gone bonkers," George said. "At least as far as I'm concerned. Maybe it's post-Vietnam syndrome."

"After seventeen years?"

This time it was George who shrugged. Then he leaned across the space between us and took one of my cigarettes for himself.

"If you even hint at what you're thinking to Tommy, he's going to have the state police in here, he's going to have the FBI in here, he's going to have four kinds of autopsies—"

"There's probably going to have to be an autopsy anyway," I said. "She's away from her regular doctor and she died suddenly. I think it's mandated by the state."

"Then at least keep your mouth shut until the findings are in. You know anything about this guy Damon Rask?"

"I've heard of him."

"Yeah, well, so has Tommy Dick. Rask had to get a court order to stop Tommy from watching his house—and it didn't work, either, but Rask doesn't know it. Tommy's out on the old Deverton place three, four nights a week, with a camera and an infrared, taking pictures of that damn place, and—"

"George," I said, "what has all this got to do with Felicia?"

"It doesn't have anything to do with Felicia. I'm just telling you what Tommy's like. He's gone crazy on the subject of Damon Rask. And whenever anybody around here dies—and I mean anybody, some ninety-year-old lady with Hodgkin's disease, for God's sake—Tommy's out there trying to tie it to Rask. And trying to make it murder. He's gotten worse than you are."

"Thanks a lot, George."

"Don't mention it."

I blew a stream of smoke at the porch ceiling and thought about it for a minute. "What about Cordie?" I said. "Maybe Tommy would be right. That sounded like New Age stuff in there. Maybe Cordie's connected to Rask."

"Nah. She tried him maybe a year, year and a half ago. She didn't like him. She goes to some lady in Westport now."

"Goes to?"

"For readings," George said.

"Oh," I said.

"Cordie's completely harmless," George said. "I mean, that little scene in there isn't par for the course. Mostly she just pretends to go into a trance and then tells you the god of the dead has great things in store for you. Or something."

"From what I hear, he's got great things in store for everybody."

"Yeah. But my point is, she's not connected to Rask, as far as any of us knows, and if you say something to Tommy—"

"Yes, yes," I said, "but George, think about it for a minute. *Couldn't* Felicia have been murdered?"

"What for?"

"You've got to be kidding," I said.

"No, I'm not. We all hated her guts? Yes, we did. So what?"

"People do commit murder out of hate, George."

"Yeah, I know. But the thing is, why would any of us bother? We've all hated her for years. We've just avoided her."

"Elizabeth couldn't avoid her," I said.

"Elizabeth could have avoided her anytime she wanted to. All she had to do was move out. Or get Felicia to move out, which was more to the point."

"Felicia wouldn't have moved out of her own house," I said, "and Elizabeth could never afford something like that on her own."

"She didn't have to. It's her house."

"What?"

"It's her house," George said. "Felicia deeded it to her maybe ten, twelve years ago. Elizabeth can do anything she wants with it. She just has to find someplace for Felicia to live—and Felicia's trust would have paid the rent. And she can't—couldn't— Christ, what's wrong with me — anyway, Felicia didn't want to go into a nursing home, any nursing home, ever. So there was that. But she wasn't ready for a nursing home, so—"

"Wait a minute," I said. "What about the trust? Does Elizabeth inherit that?"

"We all inherit it. It's just an annuity out of the family pool. And before you get all excited, I worked the figures out once. Now that she's dead, we'll each get about a dollar ninety-eight extra. There's just too many of us."

"It can't be a dollar ninety-eight."

"Hyperbole, Pay. For God's sake. You were the English major."

Actually, I was a philosophy major. This didn't seem like the time to bring it up. George was getting restless, and I was getting restless, too. My throat was raw from the unaccustomed onslaught of smoke, and I was cold. Very cold. The snow was coming down thicker than ever, and the wind was rising.

"Listen," I said, after a while, "what you said in there, about Felicia's heart condition, was that true?"

"Very true. She had three heart attacks in a row back in 1984. She had bypass surgery. She had that thing they do where they scrape the cholesterol crap out of your arteries. She was a mess."

"But she hasn't been a mess since," I said.

"She's been better. She had a lot of surgery, Pay. That's supposed to make you better."

"But you also said she was bad about taking care of herself."

George shrugged again. "She was Felicia," he said. "They told her to take some pills, she wouldn't take them. They told her to stay off red meat, she had steak four nights a week. They told her to get some exercise, all she exercised was her mouth, and the way she did it, it might have been enough. Other than that, she made herb remedies. You know how she was about plants."

"It doesn't seem odd to you she did everything possible to destroy herself, and she was fine for *six years?*"

"No."

"George."

"Patience, for *God's* sake. Heart disease isn't like a physics experiment. These things happen. And we don't know she was fine. She could have been in pain ninety percent of the time, and if it wasn't lethal, she just might not have let anyone know about it. Remember the Starlight Ball?"

I remembered the Starlight Ball. Everybody in the family remembered the Starlight Ball, because it was proof positive that Felicia Brigham McKenna had been mentally disturbed, even if she hadn't been clinically classifiable.

The Starlight Ball was a subscription dance held for fourteen- and fifteen-year-olds every Thanksgiving Eve in a hotel in New York City.

In 1968, the last year George was forced to attend, Felicia had been on the Invitations Committee. Like every other member of the committee, she had taken a seat on the dais on the night of the dance. She had sat in that seat for four hours, shaking hands with the children who were presented to her, making small talk with the other members of the committee, even drinking a glass of punch. She had been caustic, self-righteous, judgmental and bitchy—just as she always was. Then, when the dance was over, she had calmly informed the hotel that she'd been sitting on a sliver of metal all night—and showed them the damn thing sticking out of her ass to prove it.

"It was the Starlight Ball that convinced *me,*" George said now. "All those stories about women losing their underwear while they walk down the aisle and stepping right out of the damn things as if nothing had happened. All that denial. The great New England Old Money tradition. Stoicism unto death, and for what? So some absolutely meaningless ritual can go on without interruption."

"A wedding isn't a meaningless ritual."

"The Starlight Ball isn't a wedding."

"Maybe the Starlight Ball wasn't a meaningless ritual to her."

"You know what your problem is?" George said. "You don't want to give it up. You don't want to live with it, you couldn't stand that, but you don't want to give it up. Coming-out parties. Subscription dances. High tea. You've let it get to you, Patience."

"No, I haven't."

"Yes, you have. You think you haven't because you didn't inherit the bitchy side of it. You're not an anti-Semite and you're not a snob. But Ma isn't an anti-Semite or a snob, either, and neither is Dad. That can be part of it, too. The Underground Railroad was staffed and financed by Old New England money."

"Is that so bad?"

"The Underground Railroad isn't bad at all," George said. "What's bad is this schtick they're all in, this thing they have of bringing up their children so differently from the way everybody else is brought up that the children never can fit in anyplace but where their parents want them to. It's not exclusivity, Pay, it's imprisonment. Most of the guys I knew at prep school are huddled up in gentlemen's clubs somewhere, trying to pretend the rest of the world doesn't exist."

"Am I doing that?"

"Nope. You're just running around being in control all the time, playing Mother to everybody you know. If I was Nick, I'd lock you in a closet somewhere with a stack of *Car and Driver* magazines and nothing on the radio but Tammy Wynette, and not let you out for a year."

"I'm the one who likes Tammy Wynette," I said. "Nick doesn't."

"Nick is a nice man you're not good enough to," George said, "and as for Felicia—" He jerked his thumb in the general direction of the front door. "Ma's had that bunch for a week, and they're driving her crazy. You know she isn't going to throw them out, no matter what she says. I know this wedding isn't your fault. I know what she's like. I know she's playing martyr. I just don't want you making it worse."

"Meaning you don't want me telling Tommy I think there's something fishy about the way Felicia died, even if there is."

"There isn't."

"Have you ever seen anyone have a heart attack?" I asked. "I haven't, but George, that thing that happened to her hands, that clawing, I mean they started to look like claws—I can't put my finger on it, but I've read about that somewhere. That's a symptom of something specific, and it isn't coronary thrombosis. And the thing is—"

"Here they come," George said.

He was pointing down the drive. I followed his finger and found them, a little line of three cars with an ambulance bringing up the rear, just disappearing into the trees near our front gate. A moment later, they began to reappear on our side of the windbreak. Tommy Dick would be in the police car, I thought, and the boys in the ambulance might be people I knew, too. The black Porsche would belong to Chris Bennett, if Dr. Bennett was who I thought he was—a poor boy from my grammar-school days, with ambitions for big money and an eye for how to spend it. It was the little blue Volvo I couldn't place— the one that was so old and rattled so violently I thought it was going to come to pieces in front of my eyes.

"Who's that?" I asked.

George turned his hands palms up, meaning he didn't know. "Are you going to keep your mouth shut?" he asked.

"For the moment," I said.

"Try for the moment after next, too. We're going to be up to our necks in crap even without all that."

The vehicles pulled into the open space in front of our garages and, one after the other, cut their engines. Two young men got out of the ambulance who were much too young for me to know. Tommy Dick got out of his police car. A tall youngish man with black hair and a too-refined face got out of the Porsche—quite definitely the Chris Bennett I had known, just as pretty and nervous as ever. I turned to the Volvo and waited, wondering who the hell was going to get out of *that.*

Whoever it was was having trouble with the doors—both doors. I took a little time getting used to the idea that there were two people in the car instead of one—and therefore two mysterious visitors instead of one—and then watched in growing surprise as a pair of bright blond heads emerged into the snow.

Delia Grantham and Susanna Mars.

EIGHT

I AM THE KIND OF PERSON who likes to keep her life safely compart-
mentalized. Even in grade school, I resisted attempts to bring my
friends home or my parents to school. My mother called this secretive,
but it wasn't. It was simply the only way I knew to handle my confusion. Even then I tended to want contradictory things, and to want
them simultaneously, and sometimes to get them. Having those things
together in one room made my head ache.

When I saw Delia and Susanna get out of that car, my first thought
was: *this is about to get totally out of control*—and that was true, but not
for the reasons I was thinking it at the time. I was just worried I
wouldn't know how to behave. Delia and Susanna expected me to be
The Rebel, which was the persona I cultivated all the time I was at
school. My mother expected me to be The Reluctant Conformist,
which was how I had managed to survive to adulthood in my family.
Then there was Phoebe, who expected other things altogether. I was
suddenly in one of those situations where it is impossible to keep
anybody happy for long.

I would have gone on worrying about this—and not worrying about
what I should have been worrying about, like why Delia and Susanna
had kept on coming even though they were following a police car to
my house—if it hadn't been for Tommy Dick. Tommy Dick is a fairly
common type in rural America. Far more intelligent than most of the
people around him, infinitely more intelligent than the life he is expected to live, he nonetheless has no intention of going anywhere or
doing anything else. He survives by masks and subterfuges. He lets
people think he's stupid—just another dumb old country boy, New
England variety—and he uses his blank periods to good advantage.
He *thinks.*

He'd gone into one of his blank periods almost as soon as he saw
Delia and Susanna get out of the car. While I'd been panicking, he'd
been putting the picture together. Now he blinked slowly in the direc-

tion of the two blond women and shook his head. He couldn't make up his mind. They might be behaving like standard nuts—something he could believe easily, given what he knew about them. They could be up to something sinister. Tommy Dick had had a long, hard life. Vietnam hadn't been the worst of it. He thought anybody could be up to something sinister.

For endless, inchoate moments, we all stood there, frozen, as if we were waiting for someone to tell us what to do. Then Phoebe came out onto the porch, letting the storm door slam behind her. The noise got us moving. George and I went down the steps. The ambulance boys went up the steps. Tommy Dick marched over to Delia and Susanna and planted himself between them and the porch.

"What the hell," he said, "are you two doing here?"

I remembered Susanna from school as being a basically timid sort. She was the kind of girl who hid in the bathroom at dances when boys *did* want to dance with her. Faced with Tommy Dick in full rage, though, she didn't even blink. It was Delia who folded and folded fast. She was more warmly dressed than anyone else in the yard, covered from neck to ankles in an impossibly heavy fur coat, but she was the only one who was shaking.

Susanna patted ineffectually at her hairpins and said, "What do you think we're doing here? We came to see McKenna."

"You came to see McKenna," Tommy Dick said.

"Susanna," Delia said—and if I hadn't been practically in her lap by then, I wouldn't have heard her. Her voice was that soft and that wavery. "We have to get out of here. There's something wrong."

"Of course there's something wrong," Susanna said. "There's an ambulance here. I can *see* that, for Christ's sake."

"Susanna."

Delia grabbed Susanna's arm, and Susanna brushed her off. I had been walking steadily forward the whole time that conversation was taking place, and now I was almost between them. Up close, Susanna didn't look as unfazed as she sounded. The lines of strain I'd noticed in the bookstore were still there, accompanied by an oddly frantic defiance. Susanna always got defiant when she got caught doing something she herself thought was wrong. It was as if she couldn't bear to think of herself making mistakes.

Back on the porch, Phoebe had decided this was something she couldn't let herself be left out of. I heard her careful, plodding pregnant-walk on the stairs, and then the soft swish of snow and she trotted up behind me.

"Patience," she whispered in my ear, "what's going on here?"

"Damned if I know," I said.

Tommy looked Phoebe over and nodded a little. Anybody might be capable of something sinister, but Phoebe is a person who inspires instant trust. Tommy was willing to give it to her. He turned back to Delia and Susanna and said, "There *is* an ambulance here and there *is* something wrong and I think it's about time you two got *out* of here."

"Well, at least you're not swearing at me," Susanna said. "God, the past four years, I thought the f-word was the only word you knew."

"Susanna," Delia said desperately.

"Oh, leave me alone," Susanna said.

Up to then, Delia had been shaky but operational. Now she collapsed, in every way but the physical. She *became* her clothes. Coat, earrings, high-heeled Gucci boots: she could have been a mannequin in Saks's window, if mannequins were ever made out of Silly Putty.

I went to her because I didn't want to deal with Susanna in her present mood, and because I didn't want to see anyone fall down in that snow. It was the sticky kind, with little flecks of oil in it. Even new-fallen, it looked wet. I checked Phoebe out, to make sure she wasn't about to fall too, and then took Delia's arm.

"Relax," I said.

Delia shuddered. "Patience Patience Patience," she said, slurring it together, as if it were all one word, "I don't know what we're *doing* here."

I had a feeling Delia didn't know what she was doing anywhere. Maybe she was agoraphobic, the way Susanna had said back at the bookstore. God only knows she looked terrible, and scared to death. She would have run if she could have thought of a place to run to. I gripped her arm ever tighter and said, "It's all right, really. My Great-Aunt Felicia had a heart attack, that's all."

"Oh, Patience, I'm *sorry.*"

"Are you? Nobody else is."

Delia's head snapped around, so that she was looking straight at me for the first time. Then something in her melted, and she began to giggle. "Oh dear," she said. "This is terrible. I really shouldn't—"

"Why not? You won't be the only one. You should see the way they're behaving up at the house."

"Oh dear," Delia said again. The giggles came harder. She was choking on them. "This isn't right, it really isn't. A heart attack is such a terrible thing—"

Had Delia always talked like a stereotypical Connecticut tea lady? I couldn't remember. She was the one all the rest of us wanted to be like when we were growing up, but that had to do with her success with boys and horses. She'd been sent off to Foxcroft when I'd been sent off to Emma Willard. I remembered thinking it was the perfect place for her.

She shook my hand off her arm. She was calmer, and although she still needed me, she didn't want me. I let her go.

"I'm sorry," she said. "I'm sorry we came and I'm sorry I behaved like such a fool. I am a fool, really. Susanna's right. I just can't seem to get myself together anymore."

"You're fine," I told her.

"I'm not fine, and you know it. All you have to do is look at me. Susanna wants me to get out more, to give parties. Damon wants that, too. He's always talking about it. But I just can't seem to—"

"What did you two intend to come out here for?"

"Oh that." Delia sighed. "I'm not really sure. Susanna thought if we came out here and talked to you, then I wouldn't be so afraid of giving the party, but I'd already agreed to give the party, this morning, you see, and we'd told your brother George, and I couldn't cancel it after all that, could I? Susanna is just so, so—"

"So Susanna?"

"We should have turned around when we realized Tommy was coming to your house. And then the ambulance. We noticed the ambulance half a mile ago. We should have turned up and gone to my place."

"Here comes the corpse," Tommy Dick said.

We all turned, en masse, to watch the ambulance men bring the stretcher out the front door. Chris Bennett had preceded them, and he stood on the porch in nothing but a thin expensive sweater, looking like Christopher Sarandon in *Fright Night*. Could I imagine Chris Bennett as a vampire? Yes, I could. He'd been very vampirish when we were all growing up together—the kind of boy who not only knew what side his bread was buttered on, as my mother used to say, but where the cookie jar was kept, too.

Tommy Dick waved, and Chris raised his arms and flipped his hands back and forth: inconclusive. I was surprised. For all my insistence to George that there was something fishy going on—and something that could be proved—I hadn't really expected anyone else to notice. I hadn't expected to have my suspicions confirmed, either.

Chris came down the porch steps and across the lawn to us, nodding to everyone in the yard, but to Phoebe least of all. Phoebe was pregnant, short, and looked like the sort of person who would be heavy under any circumstances. Not the sort of creature Chris Bennett considered human.

"I called the coroner," he said when he got to us. "He'll call the medical officer. We'll know for sure in a day or two."

"You mean she's dead?" Susanna said.

"Yes, she's dead," Tommy Dick said. "I'd've told you that ten minutes ago if you'd let me get a word in edgewise."

"But that's impossible," Susanna said. "I saw her this morning. She was *fine.*"

Tommy sighed. He'd known a lot of people who were fine one minute and dead the next. He was in no mood to make fine distinctions between war zones and suburban Connecticut. He shoved his hands into the pockets of his jacket and turned his back on Susanna.

"Is there a *reason* you're feeling antsy?" he asked Chris. "Is there something you can put your finger on? I don't want any calls from Hartford about how I'm behaving like a fruitcake. I don't want any calls from Town Hall, either."

"If you get any calls, you can tell them it's routine," Chris said. "Jesus Christ, Tommy, she died outside the hospital and with no medical personnel in attendance. We have to do an autopsy. It's state law."

"There are autopsies and autopsies," Tommy said.

"Are you trying to say she didn't die of a heart attack?" George said.

Chris Bennett threw up his hands. "How the hell am I supposed to know what she died of? I looked at her for ten minutes—and no, it wouldn't have made any difference if I'd looked longer. I'm not a forensic pathologist. There are some indications of heart attack. There are some indications of something else, and I don't know what it is, and just for curiosity's sake I'd like to find out."

"Just for curiosity's sake," George repeated.

"Stab me in the back, why don't you?" Tommy Dick said. "Just take that scalpel of yours and stick it in me."

"I don't carry a scalpel, Tommy. I'm not a surgeon."

"Right," Tommy said.

"Just a minute," I said.

The men all turned to me in a body, as surprised as if one of the fence posts had gotten up and walked. In New York, I would have considered it sexism—men surprised that a woman could have an opinion in a Really Serious Matter. Here, I knew it was something else. To Tommy and Chris and even George, I was something of an alien life form, a New York Woman. I think they dealt with me by pretending I wasn't there.

Chris had gone past me and started staring at Phoebe, so I said, "This is a friend of mine from New York, Phoebe Damereaux. That's Tommy Dick and this one here's Chris Bennett."

"How do you do," Phoebe said.

"Phoebe Damereaux," Delia said. "Oh, I know you. You wrote *Timeless Love.* Your books are absolutely *wonderful.*"

"Books," Chris Bennett said. I had the feeling he hadn't opened one since medical school.

"Look," I said, "you think there are symptoms of something else, and you don't know what. How about what *kind* of something else?"

"What kind?" Chris looked blanker than Tommy did in his dumb-out phases.

"Cocaine? Alcohol? An arrow in the heart?"

"Oh," Chris said.

"What are you talking about?" Susanna said. "Felicia didn't take cocaine. And an arrow in the heart would be murder."

"I know what it would be," I said.

"Oh, don't be ridiculous," Susanna said. "Who'd want to murder an old woman with heart disease? And what for?"

"Actually," Chris Bennett said, "if I had to go to the medical officer and tell him to look for something, I'd say prescription drugs."

"Prescription drugs?" Tommy and George both got that in at the same time. They were as surprised as I was, although we all probably had different reasons.

"The thing is," Chris said, "I kept getting the feeling that I'd seen it before. Or something a lot like it. It looked familiar but old, if you see what I mean. I couldn't get a handle on it, so I kept eliminating things. Like, I know I never saw anyone die of arsenic poisoning, so it couldn't be that—"

"What about your residency?" I asked him. "Don't residents have to work in emergency rooms and see all kinds of things?"

"I did my residency in ob/gyn," Chris said patiently. "I'm a gynecologist. All I ever saw at Hartford General was cancer of the uterus and twats corroded by gonorrhea."

Phoebe sidled up beside me and said in my ear, "Lovely man, isn't he? Simply *lovely.*"

"Mmm," I said.

"The point here," Chris said, "is that I've seen a lot of prescription drug deaths. Mostly, I get Valium and Librium. The shrinks hand them out like candy, and nobody can convince these idiots not to drink when they've taken them. So they take one and they have a drink and they take one more and the next thing you know, they're out cold or in a coma or just plain history. Or they take a whole stack of them on purpose and wash them down with Scotch, because they've hit menopause or their old man walked out or their son decided he was gay. And then—"

"Felicia didn't take tranquilizers," I said, mostly just to see if I could get a word in edgeways.

"Of course she didn't," Chris agreed. "I know that when I see it. It wasn't that. If I had to guess right now, I'd say some kind of speed."

"Speed?" George said.

"Well, I don't mean methamphetamine. I just mean some kind of stimulant."

"Speed," George said again. "Jesus *Christ.*"

"I don't think Felicia took speed, either," I said.

Chris shrugged, that perfect shrug every doctor in the world has down pat, the one they teach in medical school. "I don't think standing around here talking about it is doing any of us any good," he said. "I'm freezing to death and I've got hours at two-thirty. You people actually need me for anything around here?"

"No," George said.

"No," Tommy Dick said.

"Fine," Chris said. "I'm gone."

He walked over to his Porsche, threw his medical bag in the back well, and climbed behind the steering wheel. Half a minute later, he *was* gone.

Half a minute after that, Delia and Susanna were on their way to being gone, too—stuffed into Susanna's little Volvo by a Tommy Dick who had had more than he wanted to take. He was big and menacing and single-minded, and he got them stowed away with no trouble at all. Then he waited until Susanna had the engine going and the car moving, as if they were likely to jump out at him again as soon as he turned his back.

When they were safely on their way down the drive, Tommy came back to Phoebe and George and me and said, "Let's go inside. I think we'd better have a talk."

NINE

MY MOTHER is not a natural hostess. She's a trained one, the way tone-deaf people can sometimes be trained to carry a simple tune through larynx control. Unlike Phoebe, who knows instinctively what to do in every group of people greater than four, my mother follows rules. Those rules told her that, with a stranger and a lot of normally nonresident relatives in the house, it was time to serve refreshments. The four of us came back into the house to find the place flooded with the smell of mulled wine and hot buttered rum. My mother can broil hot dogs if she's forced to, throw a tea for the Friends of the Metropolitan Opera if she has to, and boil water without too much embarrassment—but she's an Einstein in the field of hot alcoholic drinks.

The smells deflected us. We stood for a while in the foyer, looking at each other helplessly and wondering how to proceed. Phoebe looked a little pained, as if what my mother was doing was a faux pas —which it might have been, in some rarefied world of perfect hospitality. George and Tommy kept staring at each other and then staring at their shoes, not sure if they wanted to kill each other or pump each other. I stuck my hands in my pockets again and wished I hadn't promised Mother not to smoke on her two-hundred-year-old wideboard floor. I'm always promising my mother things that cause me pain afterwards.

Then the door to the living room opened and Mother came out, looking harried and strangely dusty. "You'd better come into the kitchen," she said. "Robert and Daddy are in there making cookies, and I *can't* leave them alone."

"Oh dear," Phoebe said.

"Cookies?" Tommy Dick said.

I nearly said "oh dear" myself. The thought of Robert and Daddy making cookies called up visions of culinary Apocalypse.

Instead, I followed George's lead and tramped through the living room in Mother's wake, into the back hall and to the kitchen. Ephram was still in his coffin, but other than that the house both looked and felt empty. I wondered if Mother had made good on her threat to throw Elizabeth and Cordie out of her house. Immediately, I knew it couldn't be true. Their cars were still in the drive, and in order to get anywhere they'd have had to come through the front door, which they hadn't. All the back doors of our house lead to are a lot of snow-covered riding trails and a couple of frozen brooks.

Mother went into the kitchen first, then George, then Phoebe, then me. Daddy and Robert paid no attention to us, except for smiling sappily in the direction of Phoebe's distended belly. Daddy and Robert are both very big on babies. They're also both fantasists. They knew Phoebe's amniocentesis had not come out the way we would have wanted it to. There were strong indications that Phoebe's baby would be born with a condition called spina bifida, that might or might not be an unqualified disaster. They dealt with it by pretending it had been a mistake.

Of course, I dealt with it by pretending it didn't exist. I hadn't thought about it once all day. I certainly hadn't done any of the things I'd promised myself to do, like getting Phoebe to talk about it and quoting chapter and verse on how many spina bifida babies turned out all right in spite of their condition. Nick and I had decided to be therapists in this matter, more than friends, because Phoebe had stead-fastly refused to see a professional. All the professionals did, she said, was tell her she ought to have an abortion.

Now I took a seat at our kitchen table and started feeling guilty— something I am good at. Phoebe looked all right. She was fussing around the great bowl of cookie dough Daddy and Robert had mixed on the counter next to the sink, probably wondering what they had done to it to make it that very peculiar color. My problem was that I knew, I just *knew,* that if it had been me in her position, some part of me would never have stopped worrying.

Of course, Phoebe and I aren't much alike in that regard. I'm a natural worrier and a natural criminal. I'm always feeling afraid or guilty about something. Phoebe is more of an innocent. She frets about her work, and her obligations to her work. She fusses over author appearances and library talks and the way her latest jacket photo turned out. She's much calmer about her private life. In the months since she'd absorbed the results of that amniocentesis, and its implications, I'd never once seen her have an anxiety attack about the baby.

I was just making up my mind to *do something* about Phoebe the next chance I got—meaning right away, since the stress of the day seemed to have made me amnesiac—when Tommy Dick came through the kitchen door. Daddy and Robert looked up from their cooking, and both of them smiled. Daddy's smile had sadness in it, but Robert's was purely delighted. It was Robert, of course, who delivered the bombshell.

"Well!" he said. "Here's young Tom, come to tell us how the wicked old witch was murdered."

It was the kind of moment that happened often in my family, and the kind I've never gotten used to. George was looking pained, but Tommy Dick wasn't even surprised. Mother and Daddy had heard it all before. Phoebe had long ago decided my family was capable of anything, including witchcraft. I was the only one with my chin hanging down to my chest.

"For God's sake," I said, "what makes you think—"

"Now, Patience," Mother said, "I know you have more experience in these things than we do, but you can't think we're stupid. It's obvious, really."

"It is?" Tommy Dick said.

"I should have known," George said. "For Christ's effing sake, I should have known."

"I don't think you ought to swear like that in the house, George," Daddy said. "Your mother doesn't like it."

"I would have known even if that idiotic Dr. Bennett hadn't said what he did about her color," Mother said. "I buried both my parents, Patience, and they both died of heart attacks. My father keeled over on the golf course at the age of sixty-five and I was standing right next to him. I know a heart attack when I see it."

"Mother," I said, "I've read about heart attacks a million times. I was suspicious of the way she died, too, but there wasn't one thing I could really put my finger on—"

Mother waved her hands impatiently in the air. "There were her hands," she said. "I saw you notice that. And there *was* her color, Patience. When people have heart attacks they go red, and they go white, but I've never seen one yet who went blue. Her lungs were paralyzed, that's what killed her. And a heart attack doesn't paralyze the lungs."

"Well," Tommy Dick hesitated, "we don't really know—"

"Of *course* we know." Mother looked thoroughly exasperated. "What I want to know is what we're going to do about knowing. Off the top of my head, I'd suppose it was Elizabeth. And God only knows I hold no brief for Elizabeth. But—"

"Wait," Tommy Dick said. George glared at him, but it threw him off for only a moment. He and George had been glaring at each other for years. He shuffled his feet a little and cleared his throat, then went back to being the Tommy Dick we all knew. This was not necessarily the Tommy Dick the rest of the town knew, especially the part of the town that took up residence only in the summer. Sometimes I wondered what they thought, all those nice sheltered middle-class people from New York, faced with an idiot savant big enough to take their gardening sheds apart with his bare hands.

Tommy pulled a chair from the table and sat down in it. His face was set in a stubborn scowl. He knew he was going to have trouble here. He just couldn't stop himself from getting into it.

"Any of you know anything about what happened up at the Deverton place when Will Marsh died?"

George threw up his hands. "Oh, for Christ's *sake,*" he said.

Tommy stamped both feet on the floor, rocking the house. "I'm going to talk and I'm not going to be interrupted," he said. "I've got something to say and you're going to hear it. For once. God only knows, I've tried enough times before."

"Will Marsh died of an accident," George said, "and you're turning into a neurotic."

"George," Mother said. "Shh."

"Good idea," Tommy Dick said.

"For Christ's sake," George said. Again. For a minute there, he reminded me of Nick. Nick's always saying "for Christ's sake," too—usually to me.

Tommy rubbed his hands together, and stretched out his legs, and stared at our pressed tin ceiling. "What bothers me," he said finally, "isn't Old Will dying, just by itself, or that Rask guy getting what he wanted out of the zoning board because of it. That could be coincidence. This isn't a novel. Coincidences happen. What bothers me is the goddamned surveyors' stakes."

"What's a surveyors' stake?" Phoebe asked.

"Well," Tommy said, "when you've got a property and you want to know exactly where your boundary lines are, you hire this guy, a surveyor, and he comes out with your deed and the town records and whatnot, and he brings a lot of instruments, and he figures it out. About two, three months before Old Will went down the well, the Deverton lawyers, I don't know which set of them, asked for a survey. So the guy went out there and he checked the place out and he put up a bunch of stakes with string tied to them, to show where the property ended. That was about, oh, I don't know. July or August."

"Bee season," I shuddered.

"Yeah. Well. Anyway, about a month after the Deverton lawyers' people did their thing, this Damon Rask guy decided he wanted a survey done, too. His property borders the Deverton place along the north end. So he gets a lot of surveyors out there, and they do their thing, and they put up all these stakes and all this string, and the thing is, it turns out that between the Deverton place and the property Rask bought there's a gap. A great big five- or six-foot gap."

"What do you mean, a gap?" Mother said. "How could there be a gap?"

"How the hell should I know how there could be a gap? There just was one. It was like a buffer zone, sort of. A DMZ. It ran all along the line between the Deverton property and Rask property, and it was just there. So everybody figured everybody else had made a mistake, and they all got the surveyors out there again, and the guy from the town hall in the land office, and some guy from Hartford in the state land office, and they do the whole thing again. And there it was, a gap. All the way back."

"What do you mean, all the way back?" George said.

"All the way back to since before the town was incorporated," Tommy said. "It was there, and for some reason or other it had been put there on purpose. So everybody got the surveyors out again, and a whole lot of other records, and they did the Rask place and the Deverton place again, and this time they checked the other borders with the other properties. No gaps."

"Our cemetery sticks into the Deverton property," Mother said. "In fact, I'm sure we bought the land for it from them, way back somewhere."

"We did," Daddy said. "And the land George has his house on was bought from the Devertons in about 1851. But the Devertons never owned that land Rask has his house on. That was the Chistleworth place, until about 1795."

"The Chistleworths died out," Mother said. "We have an archive on them at the Historical Society."

"Are they like this all the time?" Tommy Dick asked the ceiling. George and I nodded, even though he wasn't asking us.

Mother flushed. "All I meant," she said, "was that maybe they should have checked the boundaries of the *original* Deverton property instead of the *present* one."

"Oh." Tommy brightened. "That's good. I wish we'd had you around when we were doing all that. Was there an original Chistleworth property?"

"Mr. Rask owns all of it," Mother said drily, "and all of about half a dozen other parcels, too."

"I don't understand," Phoebe said. "Who owns the property in the gap?"

Tommy shrugged. "Nobody knows, I guess. There's no record of it having been deeded to anybody, and it's too small to be a state park. Rask wants to buy it and the town may sell it to him. There's not much we can do with it and we could use the money. Rask must have a lot of it. His motto seems to be 'price no object.'"

"He definitely has a lot of it," I said. "But I don't think it would make any difference if you checked out the original Deverton property. Our cemetery does run into the middle of it, and our property has always bordered theirs. And there isn't any gap. There are bodies all over that place."

"Yes, dear," Mother said, "but maybe there's supposed to be a gap. Maybe the survey wasn't done properly when it was done. Maybe—"

"That's a terrible idea," my father said. "We have dead buried there. If we've buried them on town land, we're going to have to dig them up."

"Nonsense," Mother said.

"Whatever," Tommy Dick said. "What I'm trying to tell you here, you see, is that when the surveyors were finished they left their stakes up. Then everybody argued about the gap for a while, and what we were going to do about it, and then the whole thing just died down. Rask wanted it. The Deverton heirs didn't want it and couldn't afford it. It all seemed simple enough. Then Old Will went missing, and young Willie went out to the Deverton place to see if he could find him, and the next thing we knew we had a body in a well."

"Accident," George said firmly.

"I don't care if it was spontaneous combustion," Tommy said. "It's like I said, I care about those stakes. Because when we went out there, the Deverton stakes had all been pulled up. There was a pile of them lying next to that well, and there was one of them down in the well with Will. And I dare you, I just dare you, to come up with some explanation for *that.*"

"Shit," George said.

We all looked at each other, then at my mother, finally finished with the hot drinks and dutifully putting them on a tray. God only knew what she thought she was doing. I took a hot buttered rum from her and swallowed a great swig of it. It beat looking at Phoebe, who seemed happier than she had in months. So did Robert.

"Maybe," I said, "the Deverton heirs did it. That would give them an extra five feet of land."

"No, it wouldn't," Tommy said. "The town hall knew all about it by then. It was too late. And the Deverton heirs live down on the coast somewhere, and they don't come up here, ever."

"Damon Rask wouldn't have done it," George said. "He wants more land, not less."

"Nobody else would have done it, either," Daddy said. "What for?"

"Good question," Tommy said. "What for? I don't have an answer to it. There's a guy down at the state police, Mickey Givern, and what he says is that Old Will was crazy, and Old Will pulled those stakes, and you can never tell why a crazy person does anything. But I say I knew Old Will all my life, and he was crazy but he was foxy-crazy. He wouldn't have pulled those stakes if he didn't have a reason. So what was the reason?"

"What I want to know is what all this has to do with Felicia," Mother said. "That's what we were talking about, wasn't it? Felicia?"

Tommy had passed up hot buttered rum for mulled wine. He'd been holding it untouched in his hand for minutes. Now he raised it to his lips and swallowed the whole mug of it in a single gesture.

"Look," he said, "this is Waverly, Connecticut. We've had our share of eccentrics here, and we'll have more. We've never had any real nastiness until this thing started with the Deverton land. Old Will may have had an accident or he may have run into somebody he didn't want to know, that's up for grabs. But the way it looks, the official verdict on the death of Felicia McKenna is going to be murder, and we've *never* had a murder in Waverly."

"So?" George said.

"So," Tommy said, "you can try telling me we've had a sudden epidemic of psychopathic craziness here, but I won't believe you. Things have been weird, and now they're getting weirder. Old Will spent a lot of time out on the Deverton place. He's dead. Your property borders the Deverton place. One of your family is dead. This isn't New York City. I *do not* believe all this can be unconnected."

"Oh *crap,*" George said.

My mother sighed. "Tommy, dear, I understand how you feel, but you must realize that what you're thinking makes no sense. Felicia was most certainly John's aunt, and one of the family, though she'd probably have preferred not to be. But she lived in Greenwich and she hardly ever came up here, and I've never heard her express even the smallest interest in the Deverton place. There simply can't be any connection."

Of course, that was the kind of thing people in my life were always saying. So much so, it bothered me—right through the long, not-quite-silent-enough afternoon after Tommy Dick finally left; right through dinner; right through a phone call to Nick and another phone call to Adrienne. I was in one of those states where even Nick's caterwauling about couldn't-I-even-go-*home*-for-Christ's-sake-without-getting-into-trouble didn't get me off the subject. I laid the whole thing out for Adrienne and let her work on it. She may be only eight, but she can do a thousand-piece jigsaw with nothing on it but the color blue in under three hours. She told me she'd get back to me.

By the time I climbed into bed—with a bottle of Bailey's Original Irish and a novel by Charlotte MacLeod called *The Silver Ghost*—I was almost ready to admit my mother was right. Felicia had belonged to a lot of historical organizations, including the Daughters of the American Revolution and the Connecticut Dames, but not for historical purposes. Like the English landed gentry, she thought centuries of inertia gave her tone. She wouldn't have known who George Washington was if she hadn't been forced to recite a poem about him at Miss Hewitt's Classes.

As for the Deverton place itself—a piece of property in Waverly,

Connecticut, that might or might not belong to someone in particular —well, I knew what was out there: a falling-down barn, a falling-down farmhouse, a well and a ruined pigsty. Felicia would have wanted about as much to do with that place as I'd wanted to do with her.

TEN

I WENT OUT the next morning more in a spirit of restlessness than for any other reason. God only knows, there's nothing to do in Waverly at six in the A.M.—and myriad good reasons, given the weather, not to do it. But the physical weather wasn't what was bothering me. It was at its February worst, blustery and dark, hardly unexpected. It was the emotional weather that was making me crazy. The last thing I remembered, before drifting off to sleep in a wash of Bailey's and dead Kelling relatives, was my mother in the hallway outside my door, telling my father she was going to take an hour before bed to go through Felicia's things.

I could just imagine Felicia's things, or the things she would have brought with her. Stuffy shirts. Stuffy blouses. Stuffy skirts. And enough jewelry to make even Phoebe's insurance agent blanch.

When Phoebe appears in public, officially, she always wears a floor-length velvet caftan, a diamond choker, twelve strands of twenty-four-inch rope diamonds, and a pair of diamond globe earrings big enough to use for crystal balls. All her jewelry is real, because, she tells me, she "was too poor for too long to be comfortable with fakes."

Right.

I opened my eyes on pitch blackness—and, because I am one of the world's worst wakers, it took me a moment to figure out where I was. Getting into bed the night before, exhausted after hours of making "general conversation" in a house where the one thing anyone wanted to talk about was the one thing my mother wouldn't have mentioned, I had made sure the thick outer curtains were drawn tightly across my windows. I think I'd had some hope of sleeping late. My bedroom faces east. Its windows are those tall, nearly-floor-to-ceiling things that were popular before the advent of air conditioning. In the absence of a total eclipse of the sun, they have to be blocked if I'm to stay in bed past the first hint of dawn.

I was awake well before that. I sat up in bed and ran my hands through my hair, trying to straighten it all out. Felicia. Phoebe. Tommy Dick. As my eyes became accustomed to the lack of light, I began to be able to pick out the particulars: the little fireplace; the table and chair; the oversized wardrobe. Like all very old houses, ours has absolutely no closet space. Instead, it has storage furniture.

I took the clock from my bedside table, squinted at it until I could make out the time, then slipped out of bed. I'd left my cigarettes on the table near the wing-backed chair, in an attempt to stop myself from smoking in bed or lighting up as soon as I woke. Like all my strategies for cutting down on my nicotine habit, this worked better at making my life inconvenient than at diminishing the amount of tobacco I consumed. The idea had been to make myself come fully awake without the help of stimulants, in preparation for giving up stimulants altogether. I was anything but fully awake when I retrieved my cigarettes from that table. I was walking through fuzz.

I was also in a very bad mood. I tried to put that down to not having had my cigarette when I wanted it—meaning before I was even vertical—but I knew it wasn't true. I was at loose ends, that was the problem. Back in New York, I had a million things to do in the morning, no matter how early I got up. I had to go through the messages that had been left on my machine after I'd gone to sleep—it's remarkable how many people in the publishing business, especially the romance end of it, want to talk at length at two o'clock in the morning. I had to go through my calendar, too. It's never very crowded, but there are always things on it I'd rather not do, and therefore have a tendency to forget. I always had bills to pay, and, with Adrienne in the house, I always had breakfast to make, too. I don't eat breakfast, but Adrienne puts away a couple of eggs and a loaf of bread every morning.

Here, I couldn't do any of that even if I wanted to. My mail was back at my apartment. Adrienne was at Courtney Feinberg's. If I started messing around in the kitchen, my mother's cook would be mortally offended. She might get terminal if she saw what I did with her food. Nick and Adrienne are praying for the day after the wedding, when Nick can take over cooking breakfast and Phoebe can cater in the rest.

I lit up, then walked over to the windows, parting the curtains to look outside. Of course, there was a further complication. Nobody in this house—not even Phoebe, in her present crazy-pregnant state— could give me the kind of conversation I got from Adrienne when she thought I was half-comatose. At dinner, I heard about the Events of her Day or the Results of her Reading—she and Courtney were presently plowing their way through *Anna Karenina,* trying to figure out just what Anna and Vronsky were *doing* that everybody thought was so bad. (I was leaving that one for Rachel Feinberg.) At breakfast, I got courtroom presentations as to why she should be allowed to buy a $115 dress at Laura Ashley for Morgan Duer's party. Or a $175 dress for the Brearley-Chapin Christmas Reception. Or—at this point, I always got a call from Rachel, nearly hysterical because Courtney had told her I was going to allow Adrienne to . . .

All I was going to get downstairs, if I hung around to hear it, was a lot of blithering about centerpieces for my wedding. Either that, or the very specific details of the long-delayed burial of dear old Uncle Ephram Aurelius.

I pressed my nose to the window and looked out. I always forget how much farther south New York is than this part of Connecticut, and how much of a difference that makes in terms of weather and light. At six, New York is dark but glowing. The promise of dawn is like an early warning system, letting the muggers know it's time to go back to their crash pads and bed. Connecticut might as well be the planet Pluto. If there was vegetation out there, I couldn't see it. I couldn't see anything, except . . .

Except. It took me a minute. In fact, it took me damn near forever, because I really wasn't fully operational yet. When it finally hit me, I felt like a complete idiot.

The *stable* light. That was the tiny glow I was seeing, at the very edge of my field of vision. The stable light was on, and the light in the stable office would also be on, because whoever Mother had taking care of the horses these days would have been up for hours, feeding them and grooming them and making them ready for anybody who wanted to ride. Mother always rode before breakfast—the way other people took One-a-Day vitamin pills.

I stubbed out my cigarette, lurched over to the wardrobe, and pulled open the great double doors. Then I felt around until I found the switch for the interior light. In seconds, I was looking at a collection of clothes I had abandoned, joyfully, many years before: Villager skirt-and-sweater sets; silk shirtwaist dresses with short sleeves; "modest" slacks with side zippers. I winced. Given my height and my thinness, my general ranginess, I must have looked like a stick-figure mannequin in stop-motion animation.

My riding clothes were at the very end of the rod—and the end farthest from where I stood—but I found them. Jodhpurs. Boots. Stock. Silk shirts with tie fronts and little pearl-encrusted tiepins sticking into them. There was also a collection of riding *jackets,* but I ignored those. One of them was from the Meadowbrook Hunt, where I'd qualified at the age of seventeen. I had also *disqualified* less than a year later, in a little incident involving a fake fox, an animal-rights activist with connections at Long Island *Newsday,* and Mrs. Robert Morrison Dowden's pink nylon wig. Besides, I didn't want to go strutting around the Connecticut countryside like a debutante photo-opportunity on her daily promenade through Central Park. I wanted to work up a sweat, and put enough space between me and the house so I didn't have to hear a word about centerpieces for at least four hours.

Actually, I hate working up a sweat, horses scare the hell out of me, and—contrary to what was said at the time—I could care less about what happens to either the American class system or the fox in a hunt. Riding before breakfast was simply the only avenue of escape open to me that my mother wouldn't consider prima facie evidence of a mental breakdown.

I grabbed a couple of sweaters I'd swiped from Nick and sat down on the edge of my bed to suit up.

Fifteen minutes later, I was standing in the cold outside the stable office door, knocking loud enough to bring Ephram Aurelius running and fully expecting to be greeted by some decrepit old man with a defective hearing aid.

What I got instead was young Willie Marsh.

Children who try to imagine what their friends will be like when they grow up almost always get it wrong. The most fleeting glance at the "prophecies" page of any high school yearbook will bear this out. The boy Most Likely To Succeed ends up settling for forty thousand a year and a job in middle management. The Most Beautiful Girl gets married at twenty and has four kids, two divorces, and thighs the size of Iowa before she's thirty-one. The odd thing about Willie Marsh was that he looked exactly the way I would have expected him to, all those years ago, if I'd ever thought about it. Unlike my brother George, who made himself look big through the artful use of bulky clothing,

Willie *was* big. He was *huge.* Nick and I are both tall—and Nick, at a properly-filled-out six eight, is no wimp—but Willie was built like a pro linebacker. He looked like a large building covered in brush-cotton flannel. Even his head—large bushy beard, large bushy moustache, thick black hair cut just short enough—was oddly architectural. The only thing that felt wrong about him was the fact that he was working for my mother.

He pointed to my head and said, "You're gonna ride a horse, McKenna, you gotta do something about that hair." Then he stepped clear of the door and motioned me inside.

The stable office was in much better shape than the last time I'd seen it—when its occupant *had* been a decrepit old man with a defective hearing aid. I didn't know how long Willie had been on the job, but it had been long enough to paint the walls and strip and repolish the wood floors. And remove most of the furniture. The last resident of these premises had gone in for eclectic collections of tag-sale office fittings.

Willie had restricted himself to a plain wood desk, a four-drawer wooden filing cabinet, a wooden chair, a wooden bookcase, and a little wheeled contraption, also of wood, that contained a hot plate and coffee things and closed up when he wasn't using it. The wood things were beautiful—exquisite, in fact, all carved in curving detail that was unmistakably hand done. And perfect. It made me depressed to realize both he and they might have been out here for three years or more. It wasn't the kind of thing my mother and I talked about, and when I came home I didn't hang around the stables. I hung around my bedroom, pretending to be asleep.

The chair was occupied by a large cardboard box, so I sat down on the edge of the desk. "It's nice in here," I said. "It must have taken you forever to fix it up."

"Ah, McKenna. Why don't you just come right out and ask how long I've been working here?"

"Was I being that obvious?"

"Let's just say I've been here since 1984."

"Seriously?"

"Very seriously."

"Oh for God's sake," I said. "Whatever for?"

"Why not?"

"Well, it isn't exactly what you said you were going to do with your life, is it? I mean, I know your mother isn't alive any more, but she must be having a fit wherever she is. All that *tsuris* to get you into Amherst—"

"*Tsuris?*"

"It's Yiddish. I don't think there's an adequate translation. But you know what I mean. She—"

"McKenna, taking care of your mother's horses is not what I'm doing with my life."

"Did you finish Amherst?"

"Oh yes. In a walk."

"Well then," I said, "are you looking for a real job? Are you writing the great American novel? Does Mother let you live here because your house burned down and you haven't been able to find anything for—for six years? What *is* going on?"

"Just a minute," he said. "I've got to feed the cats."

He got up, stuck his hands into the cardboard box, and came out with three of the smallest living felines I had ever seen. They couldn't have been more than a week old. They might have been less. They were mewling and frightened and happy only when he was stroking their fur.

He got a jar of milk and a pair of eyedroppers out of the wooden caddy, pushed the cardboard box onto the floor, and sat down in the chair. "Here," he said, passing a cat and an eyedropper to me. "I found them down at Deever Brook a couple of days ago. Mother died giving birth, I think, or maybe just froze to death. They need a lot of what my sister calls 'tactile stimulation.'"

My cat was an orange-and-white one, with outsized orange patches over eyes that weren't open yet. I folded her up in my top sweater and got some milk.

"Cute," I said.

"I tried the Great American Novel," Willie said. "Went out to the Writers Workshop at Iowa. Nearly went nuts. Came home. Then I read my way through all the books in that case over there, and all the ones I've got upstairs, and it began to occur to me I didn't have anything to say."

"That hasn't stopped anybody yet," I told him. "I'll bet it didn't stop any of the people you were with at Iowa, either."

"It probably didn't, but like I said, they drove me crazy."

"But what *are* you doing?"

Willie lifted a hand and patted the desk. "This."

"This what?" I asked in confusion.

"This desk. Also that bookcase. Also—"

"For God's sake," I said. "You *made* those?"

"Every one of them. Also all my furniture upstairs. Also that cedar chest your mother's got in her bedroom."

"Don't tell me she talked you into making her a piece like that in exchange for looking after the horses," I said. "She wouldn't do something like that."

"Don't worry. She didn't. She paid me six thousand dollars for it."

"So why are you looking after the horses at all? Can't you make a living doing that? It sounds like you charge enough."

"I charge just what I should charge. All I have to do is find buyers, and it's not as easy as you think."

I looked at the pieces again. I thought he was crazy. This was the kind of workmanship magazines like *Smithsonian* are always moaning about being "lost," except it was better. For all the nostalgic drivel about how much more wonderful everything was before the invention of power tools, a craftsman can actually do a much better job with them than with the older equipment—*if* he's willing to take the time and *if* he's willing to do the work. Willie had been willing to do both.

"Willie," I said, "you have to be the world's worst—"

"Now, now, McKenna. It's just a matter of time, I know. Look at Ellis Wheelock—"

"I have looked at Ellis Wheelock. You're better."

"Thanks. What I'm not at the moment is famous, and at these prices, you've got to be famous. I'm not saying it won't happen, because I think it will, eventually. But in the meantime, your mother lets me live above the office and keep my workshop set up in the back room there, I look after the horses for the morning run so the guy who comes in for the afternoons doesn't bitch and moan at her all day, and I can take three months to make a cedar chest without worrying how I'm going to pay rent or if I'm going to be able to sell it. You want some coffee?"

"Sure."

He tucked one cat into each of the pockets of his flannel shirt and got me coffee from the caddy. His cats were asleep. So was mine. I put down the eyedropper, careful to leave it on a stray envelope so it didn't mar the surface of the desk. Damaging that desk would have been as bad as inserting the words "tactile stimulation" into Hamlet's soliloquy.

Willie handed me my coffee and sat down again.

"So," he said. "You gonna ride a horse?"

"That's what I had in mind," I admitted. Then I looked around the office again and wished I could find an excuse to stay in it. If I didn't know Mother would be out in half an hour, I might have made one up. "It's been a while," I said. "I don't want a particularly horsey horse."

"You never did."

"I know," I said, "but I always got them. Mother was convinced that if she just tried hard enough long enough, I'd turn out like every other McKenna and fall in love with the beasts."

"You don't like horses?"

"I like them just fine. As long as I don't have to sit on them."

Willie laughed. "Okay. Don't worry about it. I'll put a saddle on something that won't strain you. I'll even give you a tip."

"Fifteen percent?"

"Ride north. Take the trail that skirts the cemetery."

"Out by the Deverton place?" I was appalled—and suspicious. Willie had to know what I was doing out here, getting on a horse for the first time in ten years. He had to have heard what had happened yesterday up at the house. I was surprised he hadn't brought it up. "You must be nuts," I told him.

Willie didn't look nuts. He stroked his beard. "Wasn't the Deverton place I was thinking of," he said. "It was—well, you go out there. When you get to the tree fork—you know the tree fork?"

I knew the tree fork. There was a little stand of trees in the middle of that trail, that for some reason nobody had ever cut down. It forced anyone riding that way to veer either left or right to get around them. Maybe they'd never been cleared because nobody had ever been sure who owned them.

"When you get to the tree fork," Willie repeated, "go around to the left, stop halfway, and look up."

"Why?"

"You'll see. Just go do it."

I stared at him, suspicious again. In no time at all, I started to feel like a paranoid. Or a conspiracy theorist. Someone—Susanna?—had told me Willie was "obsessed" with his father's death, with Damon

Rask, with the Deverton place. But he didn't *seem* to be. He hadn't mentioned any of that even once. And the tree fork wasn't the vantage point he would have chosen if he'd been conspiring to get me to the scene of the crime, or the accident. It was a good mile and a half away from the well and shielded from it by trees. Still, the fork was an easy access to all three of the properties in that direction, and why else—

"McKenna," Willie said patiently.

I smiled, sheepish. People who talk to me in that you're-getting-hysterical-again tone always make me feel sheepish.

"The tree fork," I repeated.

"And look up," Willie said. "From the right side. Then come back and tell me what you think of it."

ELEVEN

IN THE BOOKS I READ, the heroine always ends up having to do something athletic she hasn't done since childhood—and doing it well, because (this is inevitable) it's "just like riding a bicycle, once you know how, you always know how." I tried getting on a bicycle once, after fifteen years of not. It was a disaster. Just as Adrienne was telling me not to push so *hard* on the pedals, I pushed hard once too often and went flying over a scavenger's-hunt field of grass, twigs, rocks, gopher holes and broken bottles—and landed right on my ass. Joggers all over Central Park stopped dead in their tracks to look at me. I had bruises all over the left side of my body for three weeks.

Getting back on a horse was a lot like this. Willie had chosen a horse who wouldn't have strained anybody—except me. She was a mare with a yearling colt to her credit and a long-suffering expression on her face. She reminded me of my mother during the worst of my adolescence. God only knows, she was patient enough. The more mistakes I made, the more patient she got. Job had a hair-trigger temper compared to Daisy's May. When she realized I'd completely forgotten the signals for right and left, she didn't even flinch.

Fortunately, I wasn't in any hurry and there was no place I was trying to get to, although I did go off in the direction of the tree fork. It made as much sense as anything else. The most used trail on our property led off to the south, crossed the Deverton property on that side and ended in George's back yard. That was my mother's preferred route, because at the end of the first leg of it she could sit down and have coffee with her grandchildren. It wasn't the way I wanted to go. My mother is a truly great horsewoman. She can gallop with the best of them. On a good day in summer, she can make the trip to George's house—a distance of some eleven miles—in under fifteen minutes. Even on a wretched day like this, she'd overtake me on that trail no matter how big a head start I had on her. Besides, I didn't want to talk to George any more than I wanted to talk to my mother. Like Nick, he tends to lecture me.

Daisy's May and I went off to the north, jouncing along at no particular speed. At the last minute, I had plaited my hair into a single long braid and pinned it to the top of my head. My ears were covered with a pair of Willie's oversized muffs. My body was longing for a good heavy jacket. The layered-double-sweater routine works fine during a vigorous workout, but it doesn't do much when all you're doing is sitting still while a horse inches you forward through a cold and biting wind. I was lucky the sun had started to come up—or to do what passed for coming up in February in this part of Connecticut. The sky had gone from black to gray, except where it was jammed by storm clouds. There was even a thin line of light across the horizon.

After about ten or fifteen minutes—long enough for me to decide that all that talk about the "beauties of nature" was just the idiocy I'd always thought it was; there's nothing beautiful about the body of a fish dead in the pond water that froze around him—we were finally clear of the house, and I relaxed. I nudged Daisy's May to go a little faster. She obliged, and we were clear of the fish. Then I checked out the rest of the scenery. Trees. Rocks. Snow. One small rabbit, not as cute as the kind that gets its picture on a Hallmark card. Phoebe had once said about the country that it was "a place where people thought vegetation was a cultural event."

On the other hand, Phoebe liked the country well enough in the spring and summer, and so did I. Wasp stings *are* a cultural event.

We were passing the edge of the cemetery when I first looked "up." The cemetery was laid out in a circle of pyramids, with old John McKenna at the center and each of his children, the heads of the various branches of the family, making tiny points around him. The headstones were all plain and rather small. In old John's day, there had been no choice. Headstones were made of marble, marble was hard to come by, and people took what they could get. Then, when the fashion came in for polished granite, nobody had wanted to overwhelm the "ancient" stones—to seem to be pushing. Certainly no one had gone in for statues of marble angels or those great scroll-like memorials that make places like Woodlawn so surreal. There were just rows and rows of plain little stones, tall and thin near the center, short and long near the edges, covered with snow. They gave me the creeps.

"Great," I said to Daisy's May, happy to be talking to someone who couldn't talk back, and couldn't remind me of what I'd said later, either. "I gave up reading ghost stories because they kept me awake nights. So now it's the middle of the morning, what am I doing?"

Daisy's May made a nice little whinny, as if she'd been taught to answer when spoken to.

I turned away from the cemetery and scanned the horizon, thinking the sight of all that scenery might bring me to my senses. I wished for birds, but didn't get any. It was too early, too cold and too dead. I wished for my apartment in New York, but I knew I wasn't going to get that, either. I had a wedding to get through before I could even think of it.

My glance had strayed back to the cemetery, and I jerked away abruptly. Creepy was too weak a word to describe what I was feeling. It was so damn quiet out there. I don't wear a watch, so I didn't know what time it was, but it felt as if I'd been out on that horse trail for hours. I was sure it had been at least half an hour. Why hadn't I heard sounds coming from the house and the stables—my mother and Elizabeth saddling up, maybe, or riding off in the other direction? Surely, I couldn't have ridden far enough to be out of range of the sound of a fifteen-hand stallion thundering across the frozen wastes. Or whatever these were.

Actually, I not only could have gone that far, I probably had, but I was in no mood to be rational. It really *was* quiet out there. Quiet, quiet, quiet. And empty. From where I was, it was easy to imagine that there was nothing on the order of civilization, or other human beings, for hundreds of miles. Some people like that. I'm a city girl, at heart if not by birth. I like the safety of crowds. Cemeteries have never been my favorite places.

I had jerked my head around and lifted it—instinctively and reflexively, the way people do in television movies. I registered the flying saucer almost as soon as I saw it, but it didn't quite compute. *Flying saucer, flying saucer, flying saucer,* my head kept saying. Then some little nitpicking part of me made the correction: hovering *saucer, you fool.*

Hovering saucer.

Right.

I may have forgotten practically everything I knew about riding a horse, but there was one thing I still could do—stop. I reined Daisy's May in without noticing I was doing it. Then I stood up in the stirrups to get a better look. The better look didn't help. The saucer—hovering or flying—did not go away, and didn't turn into something else. It just sat there, its great domed body gleaming like polished glass in the faint light, its green metal rim curving flat and dull into a nest of evergreen trees.

I urged Daisy's May forward to get a better look, then urged her forward again. I did it until I realized that the look was better every step we took toward the tree fork—and that this must have been what Willie wanted me to see.

I got us out to the tree fork as fast as I could without falling off, then stopped again. From the place where Willie had asked me to stand, the view was great, and it was incontrovertible. My mother's house was behind me. The cemetery was behind and to my left. The Deverton place was just at my left side. What was in front of me was Damon Rask's private foothill, and just as George had said, he had a flying saucer on top of it.

Or the replica of a flying saucer. That was more likely, but it wasn't in any way more sane.

In fact, it may have been less.

I couldn't have made it up that hill in record time unless I was a much better rider than I was, but I made it in record time for me. At first, I was worried I'd be stopped by fences or security guards. Then I remembered that all these old properties out here had easements, letting riders from one use the trails that crossed the others. Before the Great New York State Real Estate Boom, Litchfield County had been the second-largest horsey enclave in the East, beaten only by Virginia in the competition for who could dedicate their lives most fanatically to a large, pretty but essentially stupid animal. The rights of horses and riders were taken like natural law out here. Damon Rask may have convinced the zoning board to let him build that *thing* at the top of his hill. If he'd been smart, he wouldn't have asked them to nullify the easements.

The security didn't start until I got near the top of the hill, and at that point there wasn't much of it. A plain split-rail fence, whitewashed. That was it. I looked above it to see what else there might be, but my view was blocked by trees. Maybe because the hill was high and rocky, it had been deemed unsuitable for horse trails. For whatever reason, the evergreens hadn't been leveled in decades. I looked along the fence for a gate. I didn't see one. The fence probably went all the way around the hill, with gates in only one or two places, and that could be miles.

I did some jumping in my youth, badly, because I was forced to. I wouldn't have tried it then under ideal conditions. These conditions were so much less than ideal, I thought my mother herself would have had trouble both clearing the fence and avoiding a crash into the trees. I gave Daisy's May a gentle pat, and swung to the ground.

Most split-rail fences in Litchfield County, even the new ones, are handmade the "old" way. They look more authentic that way, and everyone out here wants to look authentic. I went over to the nearest post, got my arm around the rail, and tried to move it. It wiggled. It wiggled *great*. I unwrapped my arm, flexed, then wrapped it around the rail again. Then I braced myself against the ground and pushed against the post.

It took forever, but it worked. I had that end of the rail out of the post in less time than I'd expected to, and from there it was easy to dislodge the other end. The middle rail was harder. I didn't have as much leverage, and I was tired. On the other hand, I wasn't wishing for a heavy jacket any more. I was sweating as hard as anyone ever had.

I didn't have to dislodge the bottom rail—which was good, because I couldn't have done it. It was low enough to the ground so Daisy's May could step over it as long as I wasn't riding her. I got her reins and led her, uncomplaining as always, across.

Because there wasn't any trail and I was worried about making her stumble, I led her into the trees instead of getting on her back again. They were thick evergreens, closely spaced on the ground. I thought we'd have to walk a long time before we got clear of them. As it turned out, we hardly had to walk at all. The stand was less than ten feet deep. Beyond it, the ground had been cleared into a long rolling lawn. Fifteen feet above us, the lawn ended in the solid wood barrier of a California fence—hundreds and hundreds of nine-foot-high boards placed vertically and jammed together to admit no light, air or people.

"Damn," I said. I spoke as loudly as I had back on the trail, and was about to go on, but I stopped myself. The fence might be solid, but it was a fence. For all I knew, Damon and Delia were sitting on the other side of it, listening to me talk to myself. I leaned close to Daisy's

May's ear and whispered, "Why don't I just knock on the gate and say I've come to see Delia? They'll probably let me in."

It was a good idea, with one little kicker in it. It couldn't be much later than seven in the morning. My mother might get up with the chickens to ride, but Damon Rask was a city boy. And Delia, although she'd been brought up out here, had much the same attitude toward early mornings and physical exercise as I did. Negative.

I went over to the gate anyway. It was right in front of me, and it seemed silly not to. I raised my hand to knock, lowered it again, raised it again. I began to feel like a total ass. Finally, for no reason I was ever able to figure out later, I just put my thumb on the latch and gave the gate a shove.

It opened. It opened easily, swinging on oiled hinges with all the grace and secrecy of the bedroom door in a French whore's apartment. I looked through the gap at Damon Rask's house, its redwood-modern angles, its long acres of plate glass windows, its bizarre flying-saucer crown. *Fine,* I thought, *the idiot actually lives in the thing.*

I hesitated, debating Damon Rask's reaction to horse droppings on his lawn, then decided in favor of Daisy's May. Inside the fence, she'd at least have that much to protect her from the wind. I thought it was the least I could do for her. I led her through the gate and tied her to the first tree I found. It was a denuded maple with caps of ice coating the tips of all its branches.

I climbed the rest of the hill straight to the house, and when I got to it I vaulted the low rail to the deck. The plate glass windows were uncurtained. Through them, I could see Damon and Delia's furniture, a collection of "designer" modernisms they'd probably paid too much money for. The couches and chairs were all white and modular, flat to the ground and scattered across a black rug that partially covered a hardwood floor. The end tables and coffee tables were chrome and glass. The lamps were works of art, mostly cubist. Even the fireplace had been "interpreted." It consisted of a large, stone-rimmed pit in the middle of the floor with a fluted black metal funnel above it. The funnel disappeared into the ceiling.

I couldn't see a door, so I started walking around the deck. I passed the living room and got a look into the dining room: straight-backed chairs without arms, rimmed in chrome. I passed the dining room and got a look into some kind of study, with tall chrome bookcases holding copies of Damon's books in every conceivable language and a table-like desk that looked as if it were made of polished obsidian. Then I came to a glass door, and through it I got a very good look at Mr. Damon Rask himself, cutting into a soft-boiled egg.

I don't know what I'd expected. I don't know why I was shocked to see Damon Rask. He *lived* in the place, for God's sake. But shocked I was, and shocked I stayed, until he looked up, saw me, and smiled happily. Then he made turning motions with his hands, and I opened the door.

"Well," he said, when I came into the breakfast room, "who are you? Did you come to see me or do you belong to Delia?"

There was something strange about his voice, but I didn't know what. Maybe there was always something strange about his voice. Maybe you needed a strange voice to be a trance channeler.

I shrugged it off. "I'm Pay McKenna," I said, thinking he had no reason to remember me from the few times we'd met. It had always been in a crowd. "I guess I belong to Delia."

Rask had managed to get the top of his eggshell off. He put it down carefully next to his egg cup. "Yes, yes," he said. "You look like you belong to Delia. It's like a tribe up here, isn't it? You must have been intermarrying for generations. You all look alike."

"We do?"

"Cosmic bonding," Rask said solemnly. "You're drawn to each other, you know. You can't help it. It doesn't do any good to try to distinguish yourself. You can't fight city universe!"

There it was, what was wrong with his voice. The man was stoned. Stoned and loose—meaning some kind of downers, tranquilizers, a mild dose of sleeping pills. He was completely lost in the happy-happy, and he had no idea he wasn't making sense. I was suddenly more uneasy than I'd been out at the cemetery, and with better reason. I'd heard Damon Rask speak. The impression I'd had was that he always knew exactly what kind of sense he was making—even if it was nil.

He got a grip on his spoon and dived into his egg. "Delia," he said, "is in the garden. Out that way." He motioned behind him with his head, and I saw there was another door back there. "She always goes into the garden in the morning, for the plants."

"You've got plants in this weather?"

"It's a conservatory, dear one. A greenhouse. We always have plants."

"Well, then. I'm glad she's up. Maybe I'll just go out and see her."

"Up," Damon Rask said, and giggled. "Oh, I *like* that. *Up.*"

"Right."

"Don't be too long. I know how women get when they're talking."

I muttered something that was not the protofeminist statement I wanted to make, and got around him in a hurry. If he noticed I wasn't in love with the idea of staying in the same room with him, he didn't comment on it—but he probably didn't notice. He was working too hard on keeping track of his egg.

Once I got past him, I felt better. I got to the door, opened it, and shuddered a little at the dry, acid smell of greenhouse air. Then I stepped out of the breakfast room and closed the door behind me.

I found her as soon as I got into the main room. She was hanging from a rope that had been tied to one of the steel rafters, and she was several hours dead.

I knew as soon as I saw her she hadn't died by hanging.

TWELVE

TOMMY DICK got there first, but he was followed almost immediately by the ambulance and my brother George, and *they* were followed almost immediately by a white-faced Susanna Mars and an impassive Willie Marsh. What George and Susanna and Willie were doing there, I didn't know, but Tommy Dick was too busy to ask them, so I didn't ask them either. I stood in the breakfast room at the door to the greenhouse, watching what was going on at "the scene." Behind me, Damon Rask, still in his seat at the table, was putting too much orange marmalade on a piece of whole wheat toast.

While I'd been out riding, the weather had been cold and dark and windy, but mostly dry. Now it had turned nasty. Snow almost never comes down during an electrical storm—but almost never is not never. An electrical storm was definitely what we were about to have. The sky had gone completely black. Thunder rumbled and groaned and broke in the distance. Beyond Damon Rask's impossible plate glass windows, the snow that had begun falling only moments before came faster and faster and faster still, lit every once in a while by a faint trace of lightning. The effect was Vincent Price-weird, if your memories of Vincent Price stopped with *The House on Haunted Hill.* Any minute now, I expected a disembodied lady in a white net gown to appear in the air over our heads.

George expected worse. "Jesus Christ," he said. "This is loony-tunes. This is completely loony-tunes."

"Oh shut up," Susanna said. "She's out there and she's *hanged* herself— or he's hanged her— or— and you're—"

"Nobody hanged anybody," Willie said. "You can tell that just by looking at her."

But Susanna had not looked at her, and didn't intend to, and I didn't blame her. I'd seen the body twice—once when I'd found it, once just after Tommy and the ambulance men went in. The second time, a large man I didn't know was standing on a stepladder hacking away at the rope with a large knife. I turned away before he had a chance to cut her down. Delia might not have been hanged—Willie and I were both right about that; strangulation leaves distinct marks, and Delia had none of them—but she was dead. Watching a corpse in a Gloria Sachs dress, silk stockings, high heels, and perfect Elizabeth Arden makeup swinging by the neck from the end of a rope was not something I wanted to do often.

A Gloria Sachs dress. Silk stockings. High heels. Perfect Elizabeth Arden makeup. Something clicked. Without really thinking about it, I had assumed Delia had died in the morning—or at least on this side of a night's sleep, however short. I knew enough about corpses to know she hadn't died within minutes of my arrival, but *several hours dead,* the phrase that had run through my mind at the time, could mean a lot of things. Her clothes hadn't registered. I'd never seen Delia when she *wasn't* dressed like that. Even in grammar school, she had appeared every morning as perfectly turned out as a child model.

But "perfectly turned out" at home in bed with one's husband wouldn't mean Gloria Sachs and heels. It would mean lace and silk and a long velour bathrobe. Somewhere upstairs, Delia probably had a dozen of those, in a dozen different colors. She would have worn them, too. Delia always knew what clothes were "appropriate" for every occasion. And she was too much of a Connecticut girl to wear her serious jewelry before noon.

Out there, she had on a pair of diamond-and-sapphire earrings and a matching ring. Every time her body had twisted toward the light, I had seen them glint.

I edged away from the greenhouse door, keeping my eye on Damon Rask—although without the urgency I had felt when I'd first come into the house. It had become increasingly obvious that he was chemically incapable of any quick movement. He was probably chemically incapable of thought. I edged because I didn't want to disturb him. That always brought on another lecture about the All-Encompassing Cosmos.

Outside, the snow had turned to hail. The stones were crashing against the greenhouse roof with a force I thought would break the glass. I got to the kitchen door, on the opposite side of the room from the wall of plate glass, and looked inside.

Dirty dishes. Dirty plates. Dirty cups. A half-eaten chocolate cake and a china pitcher full of milk going bad. The place was a mess. And I was a genius.

I felt somebody beside me and turned to see Susanna, red-eyed and sullen, looking through at the mess along with me.

"Oh," she said. "I keep forgetting it's so early. Her cleaning lady probably doesn't come in till nine."

"It *is* nine," Willie Marsh said from across the room, pointing at his watch.

Susanna turned on him. "Then she'll be here any *minute,"* she snapped. "If you had the *least* sense of decency you'd think about what we're going to tell the poor woman instead of— instead of—"

"Oh shush, both of you," I said. "That's not the point. Just look at the mess in there."

"I *am* looking at the mess in there," Susanna said. "That *is* the point."

I went through the door into the kitchen itself. It smelled awful in there. Sour milk does that, and the fact that this was one of those kitchens with a lot of vents and fans but no outside wall—and therefore no windows—didn't help. I looked at the curdling milk and the half-eaten cake. I lifted the lid of the garbage and checked out the contents—a lot of chop bones, probably lamb, smelling of grease. Then I went to the sink and counted fondue forks.

By then, George and Willie and Susanna had come in behind me. Susanna was still sullen, and George looked ready to kill me. Only Willie was reserving judgment until he found out what was going on. I gestured to the mess and said, *"Look* at it. Did you ever know Delia to leave a mess like this in your life?"

Susanna bit her lip. "Delia wasn't much for domestic work," she said. "She had the cleaning lady in here every day but Sunday. And Sunday they always went out to eat. Lunch and dinner."

"I'm not saying I think she would have scrubbed down the kitchen," I said. "It wouldn't have taken much to put the cake and the milk away and dump the dishes in the sink. Did she usually sleep past the time her cleaning lady came in?"

Willie Marsh laughed. "Not with that idiot in the house," he said, jerking his head back in the direction of Rask. "God, she was always complaining about it. She said he was like a machine. Got up at six. Drank some vile health shake he kept upstairs in a service refrigerator next to his bed—wouldn't get out of bed without it, in fact. Came down here and had breakfast, six-thirty. *And* he expected her to come along, if she wasn't dying. And—"

"Bed at ten-thirty," Susanna put in. "It's true, too. I've been to dinner here dozens of times. At ten, he'd just fold up and go to bed and leave the rest of us down here. Even if it was a dinner party."

I thought about it. "You know," I said, "you may be right. I don't think I've ever seen him out late, even in New York. When they give book parties for him, they're always cocktail parties."

"Maybe the All-Encompassing Cosmos goes to bed at ten-thirty, too," George said.

"The bit about going to bed early wasn't so bad," Susanna said, "unless they had a lot of people in the house. When it was just me—" She blushed. "Well, we were close, you know. And Delia didn't like going out of the house. I came over to dinner once or twice a week. Damon would go to bed and we'd stay up until midnight talking. It was practically the only time we had. Damon wasn't— well, he didn't exactly go to a job or anything."

I counted the fondue forks again. Three. "Was it you last night?" I asked Susanna.

Susanna blushed again. "No," she said. "No, it wasn't. It was never me on *Monday* nights."

Willie Marsh gave her an odd look, but he didn't say anything. George gave her an even odder one, but of a different kind. It was just the sort of situation that frustrated the hell out of me. I could probably find out what everybody knew without too much trouble, but I'd have to do it when I could get each of them alone. That wasn't going to happen soon.

To get my mind off the subject, and my impulsive nature out of the way of doing something irrevocably stupid, I left the sink and went back to the counter. Three dinner plates. Three salad plates. Three dinner forks. Three salad forks. Three, three, three—and all of it second best.

"Look," I said, *"somebody* was here last night, and it had to be someone she knew well. It couldn't have been one of Damon's business people from the city, for instance. If it had been, she wouldn't have used the pewter and the Wedgwood. She'd have taken out the sterling and the Royal Doulton. So we know that much. And we know she had to have died after dinner—"

"Why?" George said. "Maybe Rask killed her in the middle of the afternoon and then made all this food and ate it—"

"And came down this morning and started eating like he is now?" I said. "He's too thin."

"Okay, maybe he threw it out."

"It's not in the garbage."

"You checked the garbage?" George said.

"Of course I checked the garbage," I said. "And don't tell me he buried it in the back yard, because there's snow out there and we would have seen tracks. She has to have eaten dinner. She has to have eaten it reasonably early, too, so Damon could get to bed by ten. Then whoever was here for dinner must have stayed for a while, because she didn't do anything about the dishes—"

"Why couldn't she have been killed right after dinner?" Willie said.

"Well, if Damon killed her, he'd have had a witness. Unless you think someone came in, wolfed down his food, and took off again right after coffee. And if Damon didn't kill her, then whoever did would have had Damon for a witness until after ten o'clock."

"Maybe Damon and whoever it was were in it together," Willie said.

"Maybe." I cleared my throat. "The thing is," I said, "I don't think —I mean, that's a greenhouse out there."

"So?" A chorus of "sos." Of course.

I glanced at Susanna. She obviously had no idea what was coming. "Well," I said, "a greenhouse is a hot house. And a dead body in a hot house, I mean—"

"Oh." Susanna turned green.

"Of course, she could have been put in the greenhouse later," I said quickly. "But if she was put there after she was dead, there ought to be some signs of her having been carried around, and I can't see any. We have to assume she either died in the greenhouse or was brought from no farther than, say, the breakfast room. And if she died in the greenhouse, she couldn't possibly have died earlier than about three in the morning."

"Three in the morning," George said.

"It had to have been Rask, then," Willie said. "Who else would have been up here at three in the morning?"

"Maybe someone was staying the night," I suggested.

Willie shook his head. "Make sense. Delia was a local girl. She went away to boarding school. She went away to college. She came right home. I suppose she could have had one of her old friends from Sarah Lawrence up for the week, but she didn't see any of those people regularly. Why would they want to kill her? And Rask only put up with visitors if they were making him money. They wouldn't want to kill her either. What for?"

"Of course Rask killed her," Susanna said. "He's crazy."

As if to prove her point, Rask's voice boomed out at us from the breakfast room. "Listen to the thrumming of the universe!" he said. "Listen to the music of the gods! The spirit of all life is calling you you you!"

"Oh God," George said. "I just did all this yesterday with Cordie."

But Damon Rask wasn't Cordie, and this particular piece of monologue was something I recognized as part of his regular "introductory" lecture. You could catch it on cable any night after midnight, on local stations with ambitions for "ratings" and not much money for programming. I poked my head into the kitchen and checked him out. He was still sitting where we had left him, still slathering marmalade on toast, and still mostly placid. Also, the weather was still nasty. Thunder rolled. The hailstones were infinitely bigger. The lightning had gone to full wattage, exploding into great fans of red light that brightened the world for a moment and then melted into nothingness.

Tommy Dick came through the greenhouse door. He saw me standing on the other side of the room and motioned to me. The others must have seen him, too, because they disappeared. One minute they were sticking to me like lichen. The next, they were gone. I pondered the fact that no one wants to talk to the police in situations like this, even if he has a completely clear conscience. Tommy Dick must lead a hell of a life.

He was motioning me to a seat on Damon Rask's right. It wasn't my idea of a good time, but I took it anyway, sitting carefully, just in case what I thought was the chair wasn't actually the chair. It didn't look like a chair. It looked like a mass of solidified fettuccine.

Tommy took the chair on Rask's other side and put his head in his hands. "Shit," he said, "this is a *mess.*"

"I noticed that," I told him.

"Are you two going to have breakfast?" Rask said. "We have a wonderful breakfast. It just takes a minute in the microwave."

"Do you think he made his egg in the microwave?" Tommy said.

"I don't know. I've never been able to figure out how to use a microwave."

"It's easy," Rask said, infinitely helpful. "You just push the button."

Tommy lifted his head. "Someday George Bush is going to say that, and we'll all end up on the moon. Shit."

"Oh no," Rask said. "There's no shit on the moon. Moon people exist only on the astral plane."

Tommy looked him over. "Well," he said, "I've seen this guy happy, and I've seen him pissed. This is the first time I've ever seen him—" He threw up his hands, checkmated.

I got out my cigarettes and lit up. There are some people so strenuously opposed to smoking, they won't allow a cigarette lit in the house, but I knew Damon Rask couldn't be one of those. His manager was Henry Wald. Wald smoked immense cheap cigars, and where he couldn't smoke he didn't go. I made an ashtray out of the little cardboard carton Damon's marmalade had come in and dropped my match into it.

"Obviously, he's on some kind of dope," I said, "and he may be in shock, too, if he discovered the body—"

"I know he's on dope," Tommy said, "but it isn't any kind of dope I'm used to and I don't know how to deal with it. Heroin, I could deal with it. Cocaine, I could deal with it. But *this.*"

"There are heroin and cocaine in Waverly, Connecticut?"

"There isn't a drug-free public high school in the United States of America," Tommy said, "and crack is everywhere. But don't worry about it. This isn't exactly Bridgeport."

"Well, he probably took some kind of tranquilizer," I said. "He's got one of those impossible schedules—writing, appearances, parties, television shows. A lot of people who do that kind of thing take something to calm down. And then something to get up again."

"Maybe," Tommy said, "but if he took something to calm down, he took an awful lot of it today. Look at him. And he had to have taken it this morning. Nothing lasts like that overnight."

"Mmm," I said. Then I told him what Susanna and Willie had been saying about Damon's habits. "You ought to check out that refrigerator of his, see if he took his drink this morning. Have it analyzed."

"I know how to do my job, McKenna."

"I didn't say you didn't."

"Yeah." He stood up. "I'm going to have the ambulance boys come back and haul him out of here after they've— after they've—" He waved helplessly toward the greenhouse. "Shit, McKenna. I knew her all her life. All *my* life. She was the first girl I ever suggested— uh, you know—to, and she's the first girl who ever turned me down. This is crap."

THIRTEEN

IN ALMOST ANY OTHER PLACE in the country, I would have had a lot of space-age equipment and self-important men to take my mind off the obvious: that a perfectly harmless woman I had known forever was dead. It's odd how much difference that makes, the character of the victim. With Felicia, I'd had no trouble converting murder into a crossword puzzle. The whole damn thing had felt like a logic problem, and still did. With Delia, my emotions kept getting in the way. She *had* been a perfectly harmless woman. Vain, silly, neurotic, overly absorbed in adult toys—she'd been all those things, too, but a lot of people were a lot worse. Like Felicia. Delia hadn't deserved to die suddenly and have her body strung up afterward.

Cities and rich suburban towns have their own mobile crime units. Rural hamlets and poor suburban towns call in the state police. Places like Waverly—rich but not suburban; rural but not poor—don't have enough crime to justify moving forensics labs and don't like to bring in the staties unless they absolutely have to. Tommy was going to have to pretty soon. In the meantime, he had his deputies on the Waverly police. There weren't a lot of them, and they were mostly very young, but they were better organized than I'd thought at first. I'd been getting antsy about George and Willie and Susanna. They were wandering around the first floor of the house, or this part of it, seemingly at will. If Damon Rask hadn't killed Delia, and one of them had . . .

Did I really think George might have killed Delia? He was my own brother, for God's sake. And what for?

I drifted back towards the kitchen. Tommy had returned to the greenhouse, looking depressed and muttering to himself. I thought I'd let him work it out a little more, before I got to be a pest again with questions. The kitchen turned out to be deserted. I checked out all that weird equipment hanging from the ceiling—I couldn't imagine Delia cooking well enough to need all those copper funnels and stainless steel pots—and drifted out again.

Damon Rask was still sitting at the breakfast table. He gave me a happy little wave as I went by, and I gave him a happy little wave back. Tommy Dick would have him sent up to Fairfield Hills for observation—which would last as long as Rask's lawyer didn't know where he was. When he found out, Damon would be transferred to someplace like the Hartford Institute for Living.

I went through the study into the living room, and found them sitting in a semicircle around the fire, a little band of reluctant pioneers. At least, George and Willie were sitting. Susanna, who had always tended to take things big, kept jumping up and sitting down again. She had been crying. It was my own bad nature that made me think they were more tears of frustration than sorrow.

I threw myself into the chair closest to George and said, "I want to get out of here. What are we all doing here, anyway?"

George grunted. "I'm here because you're here. Tommy was at my house when your call came."

"He was?" I said. "What for?"

"Coffee."

I made a face at him and got out my cigarettes. "I'd want to go home if home was anything like normal these days," I said. "Instead, Mother's got her mind on flowers and Elizabeth's got her mind on Ephram Aurelius and Cordie—"

"Cordie doesn't have a mind," George said.

"Whatever," I said. "I just don't want to go there. I wish I had some way of getting in touch with Phoebe without having to get in touch with everybody else."

"You could always hide out at my house," George said.

"No thanks," I told him. "You're the one who says Mother never goes a day without seeing your children. With that ruining the morning ride," I made a gesture at the windows and the ever-more-violent storm, "she'll drive over instead."

"Just be glad I saved the horse," Willie said. "We drive up here and what do I see? Daisy's May, tethered to a tree like you'd gone off to take a leak in the bushes, for Christ's sake."

I blushed, guilty as hell. I had, after all, been brought up to think of the horses *first.* Then I changed tack. "What *were* you doing driving up here? I thought you were supposed to be at the stables in the morning."

"It was my fault." Susanna was on her feet again. It didn't last long.

She sat down as soon as she started talking. "I was out at the stable office talking to him when the police car went by on Derben Road. I knew it was headed for here, and I thought, I thought—"

"What did you think?" I said.

Susanna shrugged. "I don't know. I—"

"Susanna has a little trouble with husbands and wives," Willie put in.

Susanna stood up again. This time, she walked all the way to the fireplace, put her hands on the funnel and stopped. "I wish you'd *stop* that," she said. "I don't have 'a little trouble with husbands and wives.' And it's been two years—"

"You're not over it yet," Willie said.

"Not over what?" I said.

George took my cigarettes off the coffee table and went fishing around for one for himself. "Susanna used to be married. To Chris Bennett."

Susanna pushed herself away from the fireplace and came back to the couches. "All right," she said. "I used to be married, I used to be married to Chris, and Chris, to say the least, was a first-rate bastard. But that was nearly two years ago, for God's sake. And Delia and Damon were—different."

"You're the one who told me Delia and Chris were having an affair," Willie said.

"I did *not,*" Susanna said.

I almost thought Willie was going to say "you did *too,*" but he didn't. He just got very, very reasonable. "You told me you'd heard it in town," he said, "and, okay, you said you didn't believe it. But you also said—"

"That Chris was randy as a goat, yes," Susanna said. "But that was Chris. Delia was—well, smarter than I was, at any rate."

"Meaning what?" I asked her.

"Meaning she wasn't about to end up in a divorce court if she could help it." Susanna sighed. "Look, Delia was Delia. She didn't care about sex much and she didn't care about intellectual companionship much and she didn't care about children. She cared about having a nice life, and Damon could give her that. Just look at this place." We looked. "Do you really think Delia would have risked all this just to go to bed with Chris Bennett? Whatever for?"

"Was it true she had some kind of agoraphobia?" I asked. "I re-

member your saying she did, but she was at my house the same afternoon—"

"She definitely had some kind of agoraphobia," George said. "She
was seeing a psychiatrist for it late last year. He'd come out to the
house, if you can believe it."

"We were all supposed to help her get out if we could," Susanna
said. "She made a trip out every day, to the pharmacy one day and the
bookstore another day. It was her bookstore day yesterday. When she
came in I thought I'd, I mean, I thought it would be good for her
if—"

"Okay," I said, "maybe it was good for her."

"And she had people in every day," Susanna said. "To lunch and to
dinner."

"And Monday nights, it was Chris Bennett," I said.

Susanna flushed. Again. "She really wouldn't have had an affair
with Chris, Pay. Divorce is a bitch. She knew that from my experience
even if she didn't know it any other way."

I looked at the clock. It had taken me a while to identify it as a
clock. It was made out of little groupings of pyramids and balls. I
seemed to remember that pyramids and balls had some kind of signifi-
cance in New Age spirituality, but I couldn't remember what. It didn't
matter. Once I knew what it was, the clock was easy enough to read:
9:47.

"Shouldn't you be at the bookstore now?" I said. "Or at least on
your way? I can't believe how late it's gotten."

Susanna plucked at the material of her skirt. "I don't work at the
bookstore any more. Yesterday was my last day. I— well, I decided it
was too much, keeping up two jobs. And this other job I've got I've
had for much longer, you know, and it's much more interesting—"

"It also pays less," Willie pointed out.

"Nothing pays much," Susanna said. "I've got a job in the archives
in the Nutmeg Historical Society over in Morris. It's private, you
know, funded by contributions and all that sort of thing, so they really
can't afford much except volunteers and somebody part-time. Meaning me. And it really is interesting. We do family trees for people and
that kind of thing. We look at all the old records. You wouldn't believe the kind of things that went on in Litchfield County in the stuffy
old days."

"It sounds very—uh—"

"Litchfield County," George said.

Susanna laughed. "It does. It is. I took the job when I was still married. I thought I was going to be another Litchfield County Lady. Married to a doctor. Living in a big house in the country. The whole bit. And now—"

"There must be a better-paying job you could get someplace," I said. "Come to the city, for God's sake. Phoebe and I could probably set you up with something in publishing. It wouldn't pay a fortune, but it would have to pay better than the Nutmeg Historical Society."

"But I don't want to live in the city. I want to live here. And I don't think I'd like publishing, Patience. I hear the hours are awful."

As far as I know, every job that pays decent money also has hours that are awful—but I didn't tell Susanna that. She probably knew, and she had a right to make decisions about what was important in her life. I had to admit they weren't my decisions—I couldn't stand the idea of turning into a Litchfield County Lady—but what the hell. I knew a screamingly WASP man in New York who wanted to be black.

My cigarette had burned down to the filter, mostly unsmoked. I put it out in an amber ashtray that had been polished until it looked liquid and stretched.

"God, I wish I knew where to go from here," I said. "I really can't go back to the house. They'd drive me crazy."

"I could probably give you a lift someplace," George said, "assuming you knew where you wanted to go." He thought this over a little more. "I might be able to get Phoebe for you, too. If I worked at it a little, that is."

"How would you get Phoebe for me?"

"I have to go out to the house anyway. I can just tell her I'm supposed to deliver her to you, and then bring her."

"What about work?" I said. "That's a lot of driving around, George, and none of it's near your place of business."

"Waverly isn't near my place of business. If I had any sense, I'd move down to Danbury and give up all this commuting. But don't worry about it. Butch and Mike are holding the fort. I'm only going down for about an hour today anyway."

"I'll bring the horse back," Willie said. "Soon as the rain stops, anyway."

"Do you know where you want to go?" George said.

I looked at the clock again. Nine was rapidly turning into ten, and practically everything opened by ten, even in a small town like this.

"I know where I want to go," I said. "To the land office—you know what I mean. The place I can look up deeds and whatever."

FOURTEEN

FINDING THE PLACE where I could "look up deeds and whatever" was harder than I thought it would be. There was the Town Clerk's office, where the deeds were officially registered, but there was also the zoning board and the land use commission and the archives. All of *them* had an interest in deeds, too. Then there was the State of Connecticut, which kept a lot of deeds on file in Hartford, just in case. This was the great secret of New England and the mid-Atlantic states: those kings of England who had reigned during the Colonial period had had about as good a sense of geography as I have. They granted great sweeps of land to anyone who struck them as useful, and often granted the same land to several people at once. Trying to trace a title in Connecticut before 1700 is a little like taking LSD. Hallucinations multiply, in technicolor. Disputes multiply, too. As the land began to be settled, the settlers began to get pickier and pickier about just who owned what and where. Then, a little before the turn of the century, everybody seems to have just given up. Towns began to formally incorporate, and townspeople decided to sit where they were and expend their energy getting things to grow in this impossible weather. Deeds were registered with no reference at all to the land grants of King Whoever. Houses were built, roads were laid out, and the colonists started doing some serious talking about sedition. I didn't blame them. The original Connecticut land grant was enough to cause a War of Independence all by itself.

George left me off in the very center of town, a collection of great white houses and great white churches and great white school buildings that belonged to a prep academy called The Armory. The Congregational Church where I was to be married was there, set in a perfect square of lawn. So was the building we were looking for: an oversized white mansion that had been converted into the Office of Historical Districts. Whether the office was state, local or private, neither George nor I knew. It just seemed like the right place to start.

He pulled to a stop at the curb and let his motor idle—no small thing, since he drives an oversized Land Rover and has some kind of phobia about adequate mufflers.

"There it is," he said. "Find something to do in there. I'm not going to be able to get you a car for another hour."

"I'll find something to do."

"Too bad your friend Phoebe doesn't drive." He ran a hand through his hair, flattening it, but just a little. "I wish you'd get that Nick of yours up here and have him doing some of this. I don't like having you involved in it."

"You're my younger brother," I said. "Why do you always act like I'm two years old?"

"In case you haven't noticed, we've apparently got someone running around town who's just killed two people. I don't think I'm overreacting when I don't want the third one to be you."

"If there's going to be a third one."

"There's always a third one. I should know. I read the same books you do."

He leaned across my lap and got the door open, knowing I would have to leap to the ground if I was going to get down at all. Then he took my cigarettes out of my pocket and bummed another one.

"I'm going to have to quit these things soon. I never remember to buy them any more. You getting out or not?"

I was getting out. I jumped into the softest patch of snow I could find and slammed the door shut behind me. George did something to the motor that made it rumble even louder and took off.

I looked around Waverly for a moment, almost happy. If I *was* going to live out here, I'd definitely live in town. I find a charm in it I never could see in the country. Most Connecticut towns are grey post-industrial monstrosities, or suburbs, or just nonexistent. Some, like Brookfield, seem never to have been towns at all. You can drive over every road in them and never find anything that might once have been a center. Waverly both was and is a real town, a place where people work as well as live, even though most of the people who live there now either work in the city or don't have to work at all. I wouldn't have been surprised to come across a line of children being taken on a field trip to the public library.

Except that I had no idea where the library was, any more. It might have been moved to a new building out on the Old Canfield Road.

I turned away from the street and headed up the path to the Office of Historical Districts. The house had a square colonnaded porch in front of its door, but the porch was open, and no protection against the wind. At least the weather had cleared up a little. Something was still falling from the sky, but it wasn't hailstones. It was just cold.

I tried the door, found it open, and went inside. The foyer was high-ceilinged and stark, with a chandelier hanging from the center of the ceiling and a wide flight of stairs to the second floor on one side. A hall went straight to the back, with doors opening on either side. There was no sign of human occupancy anywhere.

I thought about going upstairs—it was a lovely staircase, really, curving slightly at the bottom and graced with a polished banister— but that was silly. I went on down the center hall instead. The first door I came to had a brass plaque on it. None of the others I could see did. The brass plaque said, "Office of Restorations." Not what I was looking for. The last thing I wanted to know was what kind of lighting fixtures the Office of Historical Districts thought would be suitable for a 1722 saltbox.

I went down the hall a little farther and found the Office of Exteriors, the Office of Liaisons and the Office of Registrations. "Exteriors" was self-evident, "liaisons" was incomprehensible, and "registrations" would be where you had your house declared an official landmark. Assuming you wanted to, which you probably didn't. If you did, "Restorations" would start nagging you about your lighting fixtures. I went even farther back.

The office I wanted turned out to be the last one at the end of the hall, directly opposite the Ladies' room—which had a brass plaque, too. My office was called "Archives." As soon as I got to it, I heard voices, that low hum-and-twitter sound that always means a lot of "nice" women all talking in the same place at once. Either "Archives" was the only office in the place with a permanent staff of more than one, or it was the natural gathering place for everybody else in the building.

It had a brass knob to go along with its brass plaque. I twisted the knob and forced myself inside.

My first reaction to the Office of Archives of the Office of Historical Districts of Waverly, Connecticut, was a kind of visceral shock—all those Litchfield County Ladies, and all in one place, too. Then I realized I was still in riding clothes. Riding clothes aren't any improvement at all over the usual flowered skirt, cotton shirt, and cotton sweater. They're just an alternative uniform. I seemed to be reverting to type.

I was wasting an inordinate amount of time trying to understand how I could have turned into a Litchfield County Lady after less than twenty-four hours in Waverly, when the brightest-looking of the group broke away and came up to the counter to greet me. That was the kind of room it was: large, square, full of desks, and divided toward the front by a wooden counter with a little swinging gate in it. The Litchfield County Lady in question was about fifty-five and in very good shape. Her flowered print skirt was mostly blue.

"Excuse me," she said. "It's Miss McKenna, isn't it? Louisa's daughter?"

"That's right," I said.

"I thought so. I'm Cassie Havers. Your mother and I are on the library board together. Can I help you with something?"

The library board. I had a sudden vision of myself, ten years hence, discussing the advisability of spending a hundred dollars on the acquisition of a scholarly book on Rubens for the library of a town where most of the people who were interested in Rubens could go down to the Chestnut Tree and buy the book for themselves. And would. I would have a green flowered skirt, green canvas espadrilles, a green canvas handbag and a lifetime membership in the Greyson College Alumnae Association. I shook my head.

"Are you all right?" Cassie Havers said.

"I'm fine," I said. "I'm a little tired."

"If you came about your house, you didn't have to," Cassie Havers said. "Louisa has all that information. Of course, your house couldn't be declared a landmark—"

"It couldn't?"

"It's been added to too many times. But I don't think your mother is worried about that. Is she?" Cassie Havers looked worried herself.

"No, no," I reassured her. "My mother doesn't even know I'm here."

"You're thinking of buying a house in town, then." This made her happier. "A lot of people check with us in situations like that. It's good policy if you're thinking of buying an antique property. Historical authenticity puts such a premium on the price—"

"Actually," I said, "I wanted to look up the Deverton place. You know, the—"

"Oh, everybody knows the Deverton place." This came from another lady, older and shorter and less well kept, who now marched up from the back of the room. "The trouble that property has caused is beyond belief. Lawyers from Greenwich, lawyers from Hartford, lawyers from New York. You'd think it was zoned for development."

"Nothing is zoned for development," Cassie Havers said.

"Pay McKenna," I said.

I held out my hand, and the older lady took it. "I'm Ellen Berreson. I just meant we've been inundated with inquiries on the Deverton place. And ever since all that fuss—"

"Did you hear about all that fuss?" Cassie said.

"You mean about there being a strip of land between the Deverton place and Damon Rask's that nobody owns."

"Well," Ellen Berreson said, "it's true there's a strip of land, but it's not true nobody owns it. We thought nobody owned it, in the beginning. Because it looked that way, you see."

"Because of the way the deeds were set up," Cassie Havers said helpfully. "If all you did was look at the deeds in the Town Hall, you wouldn't necessarily realize what had happened. It looked as if that strip was just there, because it was there as long as the Chistleworth place was there, and that's almost back to the beginning, but it isn't quite."

I thought about this. I was sure I had heard someone say that the Chistleworths had owned their land "forever," meaning at least as far back as the town was incorporated, and maybe further. What was more, I was sure I'd heard it in my mother's house, with no objections from my mother. That lent weight to the proposition. My mother knows her local history. She hasn't studied it, but she has paid attention to it, through years of being nice to little old ladies and tottering old men. If the Chistleworth place had belonged to someone else, and if that someone else had had any descendants in the area, she would have known about it.

I pointed all this out to Cassie Havers and Ellen Berreson. It didn't faze them.

"You see," Ellen Berreson said, "you have to go way back. *Way* back. To before the state was even a state."

"People came here and settled," Cassie said, "and staked out huge farms and tried to do what they could with them. And then, when Connecticut became a formal colony, the deeds offices were opened up and people came and registered their properties there."

"But they didn't have to register," Ellen said. "They owned the land because they'd cleared it and worked it, you see. So if they never got around to registering it, it didn't really matter in terms of ownership."

"And then there's the problem of sales before the deeds offices opened," Cassie said. "They wouldn't be on file anywhere. When you registered your land, you either had to bring proof that you'd cleared it yourself, because that gave you title except in very unusual circumstances, or that you'd bought it from the person who had. But—"

"Everybody knew everybody back then," Ellen said. "Sometimes deeds got registered just because the town clerk knew all the people involved, and it was easier to just go on what he knew than go digging around for paperwork. Now, with that strip of land between the Deverton and the Chistleworth properties, you have to understand that that whole piece, those two properties and your parents' place and your brother's place and I don't know what all, all that originally belonged to a man named Hendershot. He— are you all right?"

"I'm fine," I said. "The name Hendershot sounds familiar." It ought to, I thought. Hadn't Felicia said Ephram Aurelius was a Hendershot?

"Do you want me to look it up for you?" Cassie said. "You might be related."

"Cassie," Ellen said, "everybody around here is related. It's—"

"Never mind," I told them. Felicia had been clear. McKennas were *not* related to Hendershots. "Go on telling me about the property."

"Yes," Cassie said. "Well. This Hendershot sold off pieces of his land, a little at a time, in the 1600s, to people who moved into the area looking to build working farms. He may have made out bills of sale and he may not have. If he did, none of them exist now. Of course, it's been over two hundred years since the original registry. They might have been lost, or they might exist in some basement somewhere, getting moldy. But if you go to the Town Clerk and look it all up, all you find is the registrations for Chistleworth, Deverton, McKenna, et cetera. There's no way to tell, from just that, that anybody else ever held title to that land."

"But doesn't that amount to there *being* no other title to that land?"

I said. "If nobody can prove they own it, then nobody owns it. Or the town does."

"That's what the town thought," Ellen Berreson said. "They were all set to sell that strip to Damon Rask. They were going to make a mint, too. As it turned out, they could have made a bigger mint than they knew. When the surveying was done, all that got discovered was that single strip between the two properties. There's more. It does a little jog about half a mile up the road and cuts right across Damon Rask's new driveway. And there isn't an easement on it, either. It started out with Mr. Rask wanting to own it. It's ending up with his *having* to own it, or at least own some of it. Either that, or build himself a new driveway, and I wouldn't know where. The way the roads have gone through in those parts, there aren't a lot of them he could plug a driveway into."

"All you have to do to prove you own that land," Cassie said, "is prove that you're a descendant of Mr. Hendershot. So that's what Mr. Rask is trying to do now. Find out who the descendants of this Mr. Hendershot were, and where they are."

I could have told them something about that, but I didn't want to. Not now.

"There are a lot of ways to prove title to land besides deeds," Ellen said, "especially of land that old. We don't have Mr. Hendershot's deed, but we do have quite a few of his papers. Letters. A diary. That sort of thing. They were donated to the library over a hundred years ago, and they were in our attic for years afterward. We put the originals in a vault at Yale in the 1960s sometime. So they wouldn't disintegrate any more than they had."

"And a good thing, too," Cassie said. "That land might belong to a poor old woman somewhere, a homeless person even. It could change a whole life."

"But would the courts uphold that kind of case?" I asked her. "It's been—well, forever. And the land's been all but abandoned. I can't believe any court would find for the nominal owner, no matter how well he might prove provenance of ownership. Wasn't there something called squatters' rights?"

"Squatters' rights only hold if the owner let the squatter squat there knowingly," Ellen said. "Mostly, that land wasn't squatted on at all. And the Chistleworths didn't have their driveway where Damon Rask has his. They didn't have their house on that part of the property at all. Mr. Rask couldn't claim he was following established custom."

"And even if he couldn't, he wouldn't want to," Cassie said. "You never know what a jury will do. My husband is a lawyer and he's always telling me that. It's going to be a lot cheaper for him in the long run just to find out who owns that piece and buy it."

"I suppose," I said.

"You don't have to suppose anything," Cassie said. "We've got everything on microfilm, right down there in the basement. You can read the whole story for yourself."

"It's a very interesting story," Ellen said. "It practically reads like something by Nathaniel Hawthorne."

"Microfilm," I said.

Cassie reached under the counter and came up with a miniature bottle of Bayer aspirin.

"We keep these on hand for people who are going to need them," she said. "It saves a lot of running up and down the stairs."

FIFTEEN

BY THE TIME Phoebe got to me, I had it more or less figured out. I also had a screaming headache. The basement of the Office of Historical Districts had been "finished," but like most basements in very old houses it wasn't really a basement at all. It was a cellar. When I stood straight up, the ceiling was less than an inch from the top of my head, and the whole place was damp. The microfilm machine was lodged in a protective cubicle, and the microfilm records encased in spongy synthetic foam, all to protect against the inevitable. In the old days, cellars weren't *supposed* to be dry. They were supposed to be good storage space for carrots and beans, which meant cold and musty. It was no surprise to me that they'd figured so prominently in Victorian ghost stories. With no windows and no electric lights to provide an illusion of sanity, they must have scared the hell out of every cook who had to go down in them.

The Hendershot story was spread out across a dozen rolls of microfilm, each cross-referenced to the other. It wasn't just letters and diaries. There was a piece from a Colonial broadsheet, and rubbings from thirty gravestones. There were pencil sketches for a portrait of the lady in the case and old Hendershot's last will and testament. There were documents from the first time a search had been done for the heir to that land. It had been a very sketchy search—sketchy enough so that it would be possible to claim that the town had been negligent.

Which, of course, was the point.

I heard the patter of feet on carpeted stairs and pushed myself away from the desk. I knew enough not to smoke in a microfilm room, but the alternative was to eat aspirin like candy. I was tired of doing that. I was getting a little nervous about it, too. Wasn't it possible to overdose on aspirin? Saying I knew nothing about drugs was understatement of British proportions. I didn't even know anything about aspirin.

Once, Phoebe and I had found a packet of something we thought was heroin. We had walked around it for hours, and tasted it, and smelled it—all without getting anywhere. We had no idea what heroin was supposed to look or taste or smell like. So much for amateur supersleuths and the Great Sherlock Holmes Tradition.

I'd left the door to the microfilm room open, but it had swung almost closed again while I'd been working. Now Phoebe pushed it partway back and stuck in her head.

"Patience?"

"Right here," I told her.

Phoebe came all the way into the room, found me at the desk, and nodded. Unlike me, she never lets herself look disheveled. Unlike my mother, she's not a fanatic about it. She was wearing a fresh maternity jumper and a fresh Brooks Brothers turtleneck, but the strain was telling on her. Her hairdo was lopsided and wispy, and she was losing pins.

There was an empty chair in the corner of the room. She dragged it over to me and sat down in it, looking exhausted. Her pregnancy seemed to have gone through a change during the night. Yesterday, she was as big as a house. Today, she was as big as an apartment building. She lifted her feet to the desk and blew out a stream of air.

"Whoosh," she said.

"Are you all right?" I asked her. "You look—" I made a helpless gesture in the air.

Phoebe frowned thoughtfully. "Do you figure doctors know what they're talking about?"

"Usually," I said. "Why?"

"Because of the spotting."

"You're spotting? Now? Shouldn't we get you to the doctor if you're spotting?"

"I'm not spotting now," Phoebe said patiently. "I was spotting when all this started. Or maybe I wasn't. Maybe I was having a period—"

"Phoebe, you can't have a period when you're pregnant."

"I know that. That's what the doctor said. That's how they figure out how far you are along. But you see, I could have been spotting, one of those times, in the beginning. And if I was, then the dates—"

I had had my reading glasses on when Phoebe came into the room. I've had them for such a short time, less than a year, I'm always forgetting about them. Now I realized they were still on my nose and took them off.

"Wait a minute," I said. "Didn't you have an ultrasound?"

"Three," Phoebe said.

"And can't they tell from the ultrasound—"

"They can't tell for sure," Phoebe said. "And with *spina bifida,* sometimes the baby doesn't grow as fast or at the same rate as he would have if, well, if everything had been all right. You see what I mean?"

I saw what she meant. I was unwilling to accept it. "Phoebe, you have these ultrasounds every however many months—"

"No," Phoebe said, "I don't."

"You don't?"

Phoebe blushed. "After they were sure about the *spina bifida,* I didn't see any point. Oh, hell. I was *afraid* to. If he's going to die as soon as he's born, I'll deal with it when he's born. And if he's practically all right, it will be a nice surprise. And if it's something in between—once I decided to go through with it, there wasn't any point in having ultrasounds and making myself brood."

"You brood anyway," I told her. "And you decided to go through with it as soon as you knew you were pregnant. It was David—"

"Let's get off David."

"Right."

"And it's probably nothing, Patience. I couldn't really be in my ninth month. I'd be having Braxton-Hicks contractions, and I'm not having any contractions at all. I just feel a little funny today, that's all."

"Funny," I repeated.

Phoebe sighed. "You're up to your neck in microfilm. And you're up to your neck in a lot of other things, too. Why don't you just tell me about it?"

I looked down at the desk. There were spools of microfilm all over it, safely stoppered up in those gray-and-black plastic minicanisters they come in. The one opened canister belonged to the spool in the machine, with the grave rubbings on it. My headache had changed character. *Ninth month,* I thought, and *funny* and *Braxton-Hicks contractions.* Sometimes I think I'm more like a man than a woman: one of those people who can lose herself in logic, who *prefers* to. I could have been excused for letting Delia's murder drive everything else out of my head. It had been so damn gruesome and so damn unexpected. I couldn't make such a good case for myself when it came to Felicia. I'd never liked the woman. Her death did as much to me emotionally as the agonies of the latest soap opera queen. It was hard to deny that I'd been looking for something to take my mind off my life. *All* of my life.

I'd called Nick the night before. Aside from that, I'd barely thought of him. I'd called Adrienne the night before, too, but although I'd thought of her more often, I hadn't given her the kind of concentrated attention I prided myself on. Adrienne was brighter than the average eight-year-old, and stronger, but she needed me. Since I'd come up to Connecticut from New York, I hadn't been there for her.

I wanted a cigarette, desperately. Instead, I took out another aspirin and started chewing it raw.

"Patience?" Phoebe said.

"Just a minute," I told her. "I'm engaging in a little self-flagellation."

"Well, don't. In case you don't know, it's almost noon. When I left your house, your Uncle Robert and your cousin Elizabeth were having some kind of fight. Your mother was not happy. George said he'd be back to pick us both up in fifteen minutes, and he did mean both."

"Ah," I said.

"Don't ah," Phoebe said. "Talk."

I looked at the microfilm display and shook my head. "Did George tell you about Delia dying?"

"He told everybody. In detail."

"Well, yes, I suppose he would. I couldn't go back to the house after all that. I couldn't deal with the confusion. So, I decided to come out here, and I thought I'd spend a couple of hours getting nowhere on an impossible problem, and instead—"

"You solved everything?" Phoebe was disappointed.

"I didn't solve anything," I said. "The people upstairs solved a little piece of the mess themselves a few months ago, but the word hasn't got out yet. I don't know, maybe they only figured it out last week. Whatever. Remember that strip of land between the Deverton place and Damon Rask's? Well, it turns out somebody *does* own it."

I sketched out what Cassie and Ellen had told me upstairs, as briefly and cogently as I could. Being me, I wasn't very brief or very cogent, but I got the point across. And Phoebe picked up on Hendershot. She's quick that way. I gestured at all the spools of microfilm and said, "They were right. It *is* like a Colonial soap opera. All played out and wrapped up before 1720."

"1720? I thought you said the land registry started around seventeen hundred."

"It did, but Waverly wasn't incorporated until 1783. Either they weren't registering before that, or they were but Hendershot didn't bother. That doesn't matter. What does matter is that Hendershot owned all that land, not only the Deverton place but the Chistleworth place and our place and a lot more. Deverton and Chistleworth had parcels side by side near what's now the Depot. And Hamath Deverton had a wife."

"Most men had wives in those days, Patience. It was a marrying time. Somebody had to spin flax and make clothes and—"

"I know, I know," I said, "but Hamath Deverton had a city wife, a woman from Boston named Anne Barr. God only knows how he talked her into marrying him. From what I read in Hendershot's diaries, she was a very fancy lady. She could read, and she read more than the Bible. She knew at least two languages besides English, Latin and French. And she was very pretty."

"Oh dear."

"Oh dear isn't the half of it. Anne had two children by Hamath Deverton, and then she got what people called 'queer.' Depressed, probably. She took to her bed and her books and she stopped talking to anybody but her children, at least as far as anyone could tell. In the meantime, Robert Chistleworth bought the neighboring property and settled down to farm.

"Now, Hamath Deverton was a born-and-bred farmer, but Robert Chistleworth was a city boy, too. He was also a man ahead of his time. He came from a wealthy family in New York, and they'd thrown him out on his ear for making speeches against the King. Actually, this part's a little fuzzy. They might only have pretended to throw him out. There was an order out for his arrest for treason. He'd have had to leave the city anyway. He bought the land next to Deverton's place, and he moved in, and he was just as much a recluse as Anne. Nobody saw him except when he came in to church or to buy staples or whatever. He was a bachelor. His family never wrote him and he never wrote them. He was quiet and he didn't cause trouble. After awhile, people almost forgot he was there. And then—"

"He got Anne Deverton pregnant?"

"Nope. He got Anne Deverton, period. One day, Hamath woke up and found her bed empty. She'd moved herself bag, baggage and babies into Robert Chistleworth's house."

Phoebe blinked. "In 1720? She did that in 1720?"

"In 1716," I said. "And believe it or not, that's not the weird part. She moved in, and nobody did anything."

"Patience, I thought adultery was against the law in those days."

"It was. In this case, though, public opinion seems to have been entirely with Anne Deverton. Even old Hendershot was on her side, and he was a church elder and an old prig, if his diaries are any indication of his personality. He called it a 'great tragedy.' He also said it was better for the 'souls of the children' to be brought up in an 'unregularized but Christian household' instead of 'blasphemously consecrated hell.' I'm quoting."

"I wonder what Hamath Deverton did," Phoebe said.

"What he did to Anne, we'll probably never know. The diaries hint at it, but they don't spell it out. What Deverton did after she left, though, is a matter of public record. He took after Robert Chistleworth with a cast-iron shovel."

"Did he kill him?"

"Almost but not quite. Deverton went over to the Chistleworth place about milking time on a Sunday evening. He sneaked up on Chistleworth while Chistleworth was working in the barn. He seems to have been aiming for Chistleworth's head. He got a hand, the left one, fortunately for Chistleworth, and a big chunk of flesh out of the left leg. Then he went after Chistleworth's cows. He killed two of them and wounded the other two. They didn't survive."

"What about Anne and the children?"

"They were on a visit to Anne's mother in Boston. Deverton might not have known that. On the other hand, he might have. Anyway, he left Robert Chistleworth for dead in the barn. And Chistleworth would have died, except it turned out he wasn't as much of a recluse as everybody thought. He gave Latin and mathematics tutoring to poor boys who wanted to qualify for Yale College. One of those boys had an appointment with him that evening. The boy showed up, couldn't find Robert at the house, and went out to the barn to see if the milking had gone late. He got there just about in time."

"What happened to Hamath Deverton?"

"Legally, nothing," I said. "Nothing could. Chistleworth had stolen not only his wife but his children. People in town knew that wasn't the way it was, but Deverton wouldn't be tried in town, if he were tried. He'd be sent out to Hartford or downstate. The best the town could do was send Hendershot out to tell Deverton they weren't going to put up with any more violence. If he went on, they'd take care of him, trial or no trial. It must have worked. Chistleworth was on the edge of dying for three months, but Deverton never bothered him, at least not physically. He just—harassed him, sort of. Chucked stones across the border between their properties. That kind of thing."

"I think I can see what's coming," Phoebe said. "Old Hendershot must have got tired of that, too."

"Actually," I said, "poor old Hendershot had a lot of problems. He had eleven children, but only two of them were boys, and neither of the boys wanted to live on the land. The girls were all married to men who lived away, and they didn't want to live on the land, either. So here he had this immense piece of property, and nobody to give it to *as property.* And he was getting old.

"In 1718, Hendershot decided to become a philanthropist. He was worried about Chistleworth and Anne Barr and the children—everybody was. Chistleworth couldn't farm any more. He'd never been good at it even when he was whole. Hendershot decided to do something for him and for the town at the same time. He cut a parcel out of his own land and gave it to Robert Chistleworth to start a school on. Chistleworth was supposed to run six grades to serve all comers, then give special tutoring to boys who wanted to go to college. He was supposed to charge. My impression was he did and he didn't. He charged if the family could pay. He forgot the whole thing if they couldn't. And he was especially protective of boys whose parents didn't want them to go on to higher education. That was his cause."

"Nice man," Phoebe said.

"Very nice. Also away from Deverton for the first time in ages, and a good thing, too. Then, in 1719, Deverton had a few reversals. He also had a religious conversion. A big religious conversion. Right in church, with lots of witnesses. He'd been doing some speculating in New York, and he had a few bad months with the weather, and with one thing and another he lost his original property. Then he disappeared for a couple of months, until one day he emerged from the woods, all wild and woolly, and declared himself for Christ. Or whatever they did in those days. From what I can figure out, he made a full confession of all his sins, in public, and a full declaration of his repentance, also in public, and then he asked Anne to come back to him.

"Hendershot wasn't entirely stupid, of course. He didn't believe Deverton at all. The problem was, the rest of the town did believe Deverton, and that put Anne Barr in an impossible position. People had been willing to put up with her situation as long as they thought she was justified. Now they thought she ought to go back to her husband. When she didn't pack up immediately and move home, they stopped talking to her and pulled their children out of Chistleworth's school.

"By winter, Chistleworth and Anne and the children were close to starvation. They would have starved, really, if Hendershot hadn't been feeding them. But Hendershot wasn't a rich man. He was just a landed one. He didn't have that much to spare. He did what he could, but right before Christmas Anne came down with pneumonia."

"And died," Phoebe said.

"And died," I agreed. "I kept looking through this stuff for Hendershot to tell me what he thought Deverton thought of that, but it's not there. All it says is that Deverton wanted the children back and the children didn't want to go."

"You can hardly blame them," Phoebe said. "Chistleworth was the only father they ever really knew."

"Things like that didn't count much in those days," I said. "Hendershot keeps hinting, though, that he had reasons for wanting to see the children stay with Robert. He just never says what. At any rate, Hendershot finally decided to take care of the problem the only way he knew how. He cut a piece of land out of his own property next to the piece he'd cut for Chistleworth, and he offered it to Deverton in exchange for Deverton's original place. It was a good deal for Deverton. It was better farming land, and there was more of it. The only thing was, Hendershot reserved that five foot strip of land for himself, to keep the two men apart, but not too far apart. Close enough for the children to visit back and forth, if you see what I mean."

"Did the children stay with Chistleworth or Deverton?"

"Both, I think. I think the deal was that Deverton got his children back, which kept his mouth shut, but Robert was there on the spot to see that Deverton didn't do them any harm. And Hendershot had that strip of land to keep them separated."

Phoebe put her hand on her belly and winced. "For someone who may be physically damaged, he sure kicks a lot," she said, referring to the baby. Then she stretched. "God, Patience, I don't see how any of this makes any difference. The Hendershots may have died out. They probably have died out. Your Uncle Ephram Aurelius was probably the last. And even if they haven't—"

"They haven't," I said. "The man had eleven children, Phoebe. There almost has to be somebody alive now with a direct connection."

"Maybe. But you're talking two hundred and seventy years. I don't care what they told you upstairs. After all this time, no court is going to—"

"But they are," I insisted. I waved my hands at the microfilm containers again. "I didn't understand either until I saw this stuff. Hendershot makes it clear over and over again that he's retaining ownership of that strip. And that he intends his heirs to retain ownership of it. Then the town— in 1722, the taxes were forgiven on that land. I think technically the Crown had to forgive them, but it doesn't matter. They were forgiven in perpetuity, in consideration of their usefulness as a 'public service.' What that means is that nobody around here wanted any more shovel incidents. When the taxes were forgiven, a statement was placed in the archives, stating that the town recognized the ownership claims of Hendershot and his heirs, and promising that nothing would ever be done to repossess the property without a full and vigorous attempt being made to find those heirs."

"And?"

"And there was one attempt to find heirs, and full and vigorous it was not."

"Negligence," Phoebe said.

"Exactly," I said.

Phoebe shook her head. "I still don't see what difference it makes, McKenna. It's not as if that strip ran right across something important. I know you said the ladies upstairs were worried about Damon Rask's driveway, but for goodness' sake. This is Damon Rask we're talking about. He's worth a mint, and from what I can see he spends money like— well, like water. Pardon the cliché. If somebody tried to hold him up for that strip, he'd just reroute his driveway. To hell with the expense."

"So? He still wants that strip, Phoebe, assuming he's still capable of wanting anything after this nervous breakdown of his. He's willing to pay for it."

"Yes," Phoebe said, "but he's not willing to pay a fortune for it."

"It runs all along those properties and does a little jump to Rask's driveway," I said. "It may be a weird shape, but it's probably a good two acres by the time you're done with it. Worth ninety to a hundred thousand dollars."

"Just what I said," Phoebe said. "No fortune."

"To you it might not be a fortune," I said, "but to other people in other circumstances, it might be different."

"Who?" Phoebe demanded. "And what's it supposed to explain? That old man who died in the well with all the surveying stakes beside him? Your Great-Aunt Felicia? Your friend Delia? What?"

"I don't know," I said.

"We don't even know your aunt was murdered yet, not for sure. We don't know anything. I like a puzzle just as much as you do, Patience—"

"More," I reminded her.

"Maybe more," she agreed. "But you've got to make sense. This is just a lot of mush with nothing to connect it at all."

I looked at all the miles and miles of microfilm, and then at the machine. "Take a look at that," I said. "It's a little hard to read, but it's a kick."

"What is it?" Phoebe got out of her chair and waddled over to squint at the screen.

"It's a rubbing of Anne Barr Deverton's tombstone," I said. "It says, 'Anne Barr Deverton, Beloved Wife of Hamath Deverton, Beloved Mistress of Robert Chistleworth.' The lady had a lot of nerve."

SIXTEEN

WE DECIDED TO GO OUT the back way—not because I was having more neurotic fantasies about Litchfield County Ladies (although I was), but because it had occurred to me that the story of Delia Grantham's murder had probably hit the radio news. The story of my own involvement might not have, but I couldn't count on that. In small towns, gossip is an obligation. To have been witness to the kind of scene I had been witness to, and not to have reported it, was mortal sin. But I hadn't wanted to talk about Delia before, and I didn't want to talk about her now. I certainly didn't want to leave myself open to the recriminations of women feeling terminally left out. Then there would be the question of just how much to tell. That Delia hadn't really died by hanging? That Damon was in the middle of some kind of nervous breakdown? That Tommy Dick was ready to call in the state police? I wouldn't have been able to decide. It was easier to find an alternate route.

The alternate route was up a steep flight of cement stairs and through a fire door. I had to help Phoebe up the stairs, and then I had to open the fire door very carefully, in case pushing too hard at it set off an alarm. If it did, it wasn't the kind you could hear, and that was all I asked for. An alarm might be going off, out of earshot, down at the fire station. I didn't care. We'd be well out of the way when the hook and ladders arrived.

George was waiting for us at the curb, motor idling, steam coming out of his ears as well as out of his engine. I helped Phoebe through the snow and into the front seat, then climbed into the back myself. The back was full of junk: an open toolbox; four planks of unfinished cedar wood; a little canvas Bonwit Teller bag with a matching Bonwit Teller thermos. Then there was the floor decor, the inevitable Ronald McDonald memorial paper sculptures. Waverly doesn't allow fast-food restaurants within its borders, and the nearest McDonald's is out on Route 69 in Watertown, but the needs of Jeeps and pickup trucks are not to be denied. They demand french-fries cartons. They get french-fries cartons.

I plunged my boots into the debris and got out my cigarettes. "It's a mess back here," I said. "What are you doing to yourself?"

"What do you mean, what am I doing to myself?" George said. "I'm not doing anything to myself. Your parents and your friends are driving me crazy."

"Big Macs and Bonwit Teller?" I asked.

"The Bonwit Teller bag is Susanna's lunch," George said. "She forgot it at home and needed somebody to bring it out to her in Morris. Me. The wood belongs to Willie Marsh. He needed somebody to pick it up from the lumber yard for him. Also me. As for the Big Macs—"

"Yes?"

"They're not Big Macs. They're Happy Meals. I have three children, Patience."

He did indeed have three children, and I hadn't seen any of them yet on this trip. I found a pack of Mamma Leone matches left over from the last time Phoebe had pregnancy cravings and got my cigarette lit. George had started the car. We were rolling out onto the two-lane blacktop, moving at an unbelievably slow speed. In my experience, George tends to think "speed limit" means the number on the dashboard above which the little red indicator will not go.

The ashtray was full of solidified chewing gum, so I picked up a Quarter-Pounder-with-Cheese box and used that instead. The town was rolling by, and Phoebe seemed to be falling asleep in the front seat. I thought that was a good idea. You're supposed to sleep a lot when you're pregnant. Phoebe never seemed to sleep at all. She either stayed up all night worrying about the baby, or stayed up all night fantasizing about how everything was going to be all right. She'd probably been smart not to have those extra ultrasounds.

We dropped into the little depression that was the Depot and passed the Chestnut Tree, its parking lot almost empty. The gas station on the other side of the road was empty, too—no Tommy Dick filling up, and no pimply high school boys wandering aimlessly around with greasy rags in their hands. The weather had finally let up for real. It was cold. It was dark. It was wet. It was not raining, snowing, sleeting, hailing, or giving off fireworks.

As we were starting up the hill to go north on 49, we hit a bump.

The bump jogged Phoebe so that her head fell a little to one side. That seemed to wake George out of his total-driver trance. He pushed Phoebe's head gently back onto the headrest and said, "Pay? I know I said I'd get you a car. I know I said that. But I couldn't."

"That's okay," I said. "I have to go home sometime."

"Yeah," George said. "Well, now's the time. Ma's driving me nuts. After I get Susanna her lunch, I'm supposed to go out to Waterbury and pick up thirty-four pounds of Jordan almonds. What in hell does she want thirty-four pounds of Jordan almonds for?"

"They go in the wedding favors," I said.

"Great," he said. "I hate Jordan almonds."

He lapsed into silence again, and I thought we were going to ride that way the rest of the trip. Instead, just as we turned onto the Old Canfield Road, he asked to bum another cigarette. I passed it to him lit. He took quick drags off it and said, "Tommy Dick called."

"Did he?" Actually, that was better news than I'd expected. I thought Nick might have called. Damon Rask was a famous man. Once his wife's death hit the news, it was really going to hit—nationwide. Nick was no fool. He was going to hear the name of the town, and he was going to know I was involved in it. *And* he was going to be furious.

My cigarette had gone out, so I lit another one. I always chain-smoke when I'm nervous. I licked my fingers and wet the match so it wouldn't burn anything down and tossed it into the Quarter-Pounder box with the rest of the debris.

"So," I said, "what did Tommy Dick want? Did he have the results of the autopsy?"

"Already?"

"Felicia's autopsy."

"Oh, that," George said. "He didn't say anything about that. This was, I don't know, maybe an hour ago. About the time I was picking up Phoebe."

"And?"

George took a drag, stared at the tip of his cigarette, took another drag, stared at the tip of his cigarette again. "I don't know," he said finally. "I picked up the phone because I happened to be standing next to it. I was in the kitchen trying to get away from all the din. Robert and Elizabeth were having some kind of argument."

"Phoebe mentioned something about that," I said.

"Did she mention what it was about? I couldn't figure it."

"She just said they were fighting."

"She probably didn't know what it was about either." George sighed. "If it wasn't for the kids, I think I'd move down to Danbury. Just to get away from all this crap. I mean, for God's sake, Pay. Except for Robert and Dad, they can't stand each other. And they can't stand us, either. What are they doing up here all the time?"

"Not standing us in person," I said.

"Right," George said. "I wish Ma had the spine to throw them out. And don't tell me Ma has more spine than anyone you know. She's a complete jellyfish when it comes to the McKennas."

"You want to tell me what Tommy Dick had on his mind?"

Now it was George's cigarette that was out. He put up his hand, and I put the pack and the matches into it.

"Tommy Dick," he said, "isn't going to call in the state police, because it isn't going to be necessary. That was the gist of the message."

"That was it?"

"That was it."

"He didn't say why?"

"He didn't say much of anything. I thought he was going to ask to talk to you, or at least to Mother. What the hell did he want to talk to me for? But he didn't ask for me, and he didn't ask for anybody else. He just said he wanted us to know we didn't have to worry. We weren't sleeping in the same house with a homicidal maniac. The whole thing was wrapped up, and if it wasn't, it would be in a day or two. He had his man."

I thought this over. "The only way that makes sense," I said, "is if he means he's going to arrest Damon Rask. But that doesn't make sense, because he'd be saying Rask was responsible for Felicia dying. Unless he did get the autopsy report, and Felicia wasn't murdered after all. But if that's the case, why didn't he—"

"Don't," George said. "You're giving me a headache."

"I'm just trying to decipher this, George."

"Yeah, well. Decipher it to Mother. Or to Phoebe here when she wakes up. I've got to deliver lunches, I've got to pick up almonds, then I've got to go smash a Toyota into a telephone pole."

"What?"

"It's got a bent bumper. I need to get it straightened out."

"So you're going to smash it into a telephone pole?"

"That's the way it's done, Patience. Only don't tell the customers that. They get nervous."

We'd come to our gate. George got out, opened up, got back in and drove through. On the other side, he repeated the process. I found myself wondering why we bothered with it. Nobody came this far down the Old Canfield Road unless they were looking for us. Even lost people gave up miles before they reached our gate. There wasn't anybody we wanted to keep out—or both wanted and were willing to —so what was the point?

We went through the stand of trees, then headed for the little circular drive in front of the porch. No parking for George—he didn't intend to hang around. I opened my window and tossed my cigarette into the snow. I was more concerned about starting a fire in all that paper than I was about a little litter on the lawn. Then we pulled to a stop, and I started gathering up the little pieces of paper I'd made notes on in the basement of the Office of Historical Districts. God only knew what I wanted them for.

In the front seat, Phoebe stirred, stretched, and sat up a little. She looked out the window on her side and shook her head. Then she said, "Patience? What day is it?"

"It's Tuesday," I said. "Why?"

"Well," she said, "here we are, arriving at your house. And there your mother is, waiting for us on the porch."

I jerked forward and looked out the window for myself. My mother was indeed waiting on the porch. Her Litchfield County Lady uniform was aquamarine. Her jacket was nowhere in sight. Her arms were folded across her chest.

She did not look calm.

In the driver's seat, my brother George decided his own cigarettes were better than mine. They were stronger. They had no filters. They were on a part of the dashboard that required him to look *away* from the house if he was going to pick them up. He got one into his mouth, materialized a lighter the way The Amazing Kreskin materialized silk scarves, and said through a cloud of smoke,

"Get out of here. I'm not even going to turn the engine off. You can spend *your* day dealing with that."

Calling my mother a "that" to be "dealt with" isn't accurate. Unlike her McKenna relatives-in-law, she keeps her head. She was keeping it now, even though she preferred freezing to death to taking on whatever was happening in the house. George gunned off as soon as I got Phoebe to the ground and the passenger door closed, but by then Mother was off the porch anyway. Phoebe not only felt funny, she *looked* funny—white, and nauseated, and a little glassy-eyed. I had her by the left arm, guiding her up the walk. The weather had been so awful for so long, nobody had had a chance to do much about ground ice. There was fresh rock salt on the path. That was it. It had done as much good as a voodoo incantation.

Mother slid a little when she came off the porch steps, but she righted herself immediately. By the time she reached Phoebe, she was standing as solidly as if what was under her feet was patterned rubber. *Dry* patterned rubber. She took Phoebe's right arm and bent down to look into her eyes. Phoebe grinned weakly—one natural mother to another.

"Oh dear," my mother said. She straightened up again. "Patience, have you any idea how long this has been going on? Has she been doing it at regular intervals?"

"Doing what?" I said.

"I'm all right," Phoebe said. "I just feel a little funny."

"Yes, dear." Mother gave her a bright, reassuring smile—so false, it startled me. "What I need to know, dear, is how *often* you've been feeling funny. Every ten minutes? Every half hour?"

"Oh my *God,*" I said.

"I felt funny in the library," Phoebe said. "That was, what, maybe half an hour ago, maybe forty-five minutes. And I felt funny here before George came. You remember. It was when Elizabeth came down and said I looked like a—"

"Never mind what Elizabeth said. Silly idiot." Mother ran a hand through her hair, already spiky-punk from having hands run through it. She also relaxed enough to notice how cold it was. The wind was rising again, and it went right through the loose weave of her cotton sweater. "It's all right," she said, "it's just false labor. But if she's got false labor now, it isn't going to be so long before she has the real thing, and we should start making plans—"

"Mother," I said, "she's only seven months pregnant."

Mother gave me a look that seemed to question just how attentive I'd been in my biology classes. Or even if I'd taken biology classes. "People do have seventh-month babies," she said, "and even with all the equipment we've got these days, predicting delivery dates is not an exact science. The doctor could have made a mistake. The baby may just be coming early. False labor usually shows up two to four weeks before the real thing. Phoebe may still be here when the real thing starts. All her support services are in New York, too. And we have a damaged child here—"

"Louisa."

Mother patted Phoebe's hand. "There, there, dear. I know. You're trying not to think about that. But we *have* to think about it if we're going to make sensible arrangements."

"Why don't we all just go back to New York," I said. "We could have my wedding at City Hall. Phoebe would be near her doctor."

"And I'd be stuck with twenty thousand dollars' worth of roses," Mother said. *"No* thank you, dear. This isn't an emergency. Not yet."

"Is that?" I pointed to the house.

Mother turned to look at the front door, faintly puzzled. In all her worry about Phoebe, she'd forgotten why she'd come outside. Now she squared her shoulders and shook her head vigorously, the picture of a Litchfield County Lady on the warpath.

"Oh, *them,*" she said. "I don't know what I'm going to do about *them.* They're driving me out of my mind."

Phoebe's "funny" feeling was all gone. She had straightened up and brightened up, and she was distinctly interested in my mother's tone of voice. There are warpaths and warpaths. The high road is high dudgeon: the kind of reaction you have to something so impossibly rude, so impossibly stupid, so impossibly malicious, you barely know how to talk about it. The low road is more like contempt. You take it when people around you are behaving like bad-tempered children.

Phoebe peeked curiously around my mother's shoulders. "What are *they* doing?" she said. "Burning the house down? Fighting over money?"

Mother sighed. "They were reading tarot cards," she said. "Or Cordie was. Dr. Bennett is in there. He came over to make sure Cordie didn't have any, uh, long-lasting effects from her little incident of yesterday afternoon. When I came out here, Cordie was offering to tell his fortune."

"Was he taking her up on it?" I asked.

"I really wouldn't know," Mother said. "I didn't stay around to find out. Although I suppose I ought to go back in."

SEVENTEEN

THEY WERE IN THE LIBRARY, the whole lot of them, a little clot of mismatched people I was beginning to think of as The Siamese Group. Except for Chris Bennett, they were always together—and Chris's position was made clear, even in this informal gathering, by his seat in a corner chair. The library could be reached from the foyer by going in the direction opposite the bedroom wing. I had to go down a short hallway lined with steel engravings of once-legendary McKenna women, but I didn't have to pass through any other rooms. Mother and Phoebe were more interested in Phoebe's condition than in anything Cordie might be doing. I left them behind in the foyer and went to find out what the fuss was about for myself. I didn't want to think about Phoebe's condition. If a baby was about to land in my lap two months before I was ready for it, I'd rather not have oodles of advance warning.

The library door was standing open when I walked up to it. I was still wearing my riding boots, but there was a runner rug in the hallway and no creaking board. Unintentionally, I made my approach in absolute silence. Cordie was seated in a wing-backed chair with her feet stretched out on a matching ottoman, her body covered from breasts to toes in a heavy-knit pink-and-white afghan. She had a breakfast tray on her lap with a lot of oversized cards spread across it. She had her hands folded in her lap and a bright, expectant look on her face. It was the look I had always associated with her—eager and sly, as if she understood only too well that people thought she was stupid and, thinking that, said things to her they shouldn't have said to anyone. Cordie always knew everybody else's secrets. I'd never thought of that before, but it was true. The knowing gave her an air of belonging Chris would just never have.

Chris, Chris, Chris. It was Chris who had caught my attention when I first came to the door, and I suddenly understood why. Like most people, I tend to believe what I see on the surface. In most situations, doing anything else is too much work. Superficially, Chris was a Changed Man from our days in grammar school together. He dressed not only well but expensively—no more Goodwill special editions for Chris—and his years at Amherst and Yale had given him a polish that made him seem more like the part of town he'd always wanted to belong to than the part of town he'd been brought up in. His looks helped. He was a handsome man, flashy-handsome, like a Christopher Sarandon or a young Peter Fonda. He had an instinct for Litchfield County style, too. Even in the days when his mother had been putting away every cent she had for Chris's education, and there'd been nothing left over to dress him with, Chris had managed to look more Ivy, more preppy, more old-old-old-old money than anybody else.

And that had been enough—for the rest of us. Waverly really *isn't* a divided town. None of us had ever been allowed to "make distinctions" on the basis of family money. Every girl I knew, rich and poor, had had a crush on Chris Bennett. He'd been invited to every party, included in every prank, elected to every secret club. I would have said he was one of the most popular boys in town, with everything that entails, in power and prestige, in the world of adolescents. Chris Bennett hadn't merely belonged. He'd been at the head of that small clique that defines "belonging" for everyone else.

Now it occurred to me that this might not have been the situation as *Chris* saw it. After all, when all his friends went away to prep school, he had stayed behind at the local high. When they'd gone off to Paris or London for the summer, he'd worked road crews to make spending money. While they attended subscription dances and coming-out parties, he studied. I could see why he'd married Susanna Mars, even though anyone who knew both of them knew they wouldn't be compatible. She was old money, old Waverly, old Litchfield County. Her roots went so far back, they were unquestionable.

I thought I knew why Susanna had married Chris, too: he was a doctor. Being old money wasn't the same thing as *having* old money, or any other kind. Susanna's people had had enough to send her to Foxcroft and Bennington, but the impression I'd had was that there wasn't going to be much left over after that. Too many generations of irresponsible eccentrics had gone through too much capital in too many ingenious ways. Since Susanna was an irresponsible eccentric herself, she was going to need somebody to keep her in Laura Ashley.

On the other side of the library, Elizabeth looked up, caught sight of me, and blinked. Then she stood and brushed imaginary wrinkles out of her skirt. "Oh God," she said. "There you are, and you want to go *riding.*"

It must have been a signal. The rest of them came to life. Daddy and Uncle Robert got up automatically. They had been trained by a ferocious maiden aunt to stand whenever a woman entered the room. Since I was getting married, I qualified as a woman. Chris got up more slowly, watching the other two. Manners had gone through so many sea changes in recent years, he didn't know how to behave. Why should he? None of the rest of us did, either.

I looked down at my clothes and decided that Elizabeth was, once again, being a twit. Anybody could see I'd already been out in them. They were a mess. I went in and sat down in the only available seat, so close to the fire my face immediately began to burn. I've never understood why my family insists on lighting fires in any room with a fireplace in it. Half the time the rooms are too small, the fires are too hot, and the effects are sweaty.

The peripatetic Siamese might have been engaged in something intense and unpleasant when Mother left them, but now they weren't engaged in anything at all. Once everybody had resettled in their seats, they didn't know what to do. They looked at each other. They looked at me. Cordie gathered up her Tarot cards and shuffled them. Nobody had anything to say.

When Cordie had the cards all shuffled, she put them down in the middle of the breakfast tray and smiled at me. "I was telling fortunes," she said. "I could tell yours."

"I don't want you to," I said. "I'm getting married. I think the future of it ought to be a surprise."

Cordie shook her head. There was nothing left of the trance-state, or the fanaticism, of the day before. She had passed through it the way a car passes through a limited local shower on a long stretch of superhighway. She picked up the cards again and tapped them into order. They'd been in as much order as they could get before.

"Everybody wants the future to be a surprise," she said. "I don't see why. You're not prepared for surprises. They sneak up on you. And that's when you make mistakes."

"I'd make mistakes anyway, Cordie," I said. "I'm not all that well organized."

"That's what I keep trying to tell her." Robert was leaning forward, in the most serious mood I'd ever seen him in. "All this—stuff—she's involved in. It doesn't really help. It just gets her agitated."

"I know you think I had some kind of breakdown yesterday," Cordie said, "but it isn't true. I was channeling, that's all. I can't control channeling. It isn't up to me. I leave the door to my soul open all the time, and the spirit comes on me when it wants to. When *she* wants to."

"Oh, *Cordie,*" Elizabeth said.

Chris Bennett suppressed a smile, but not very well.

I reached into my pocket for my cigarettes, realized I'd left them in George's car, and took one from the courtesy box my mother kept on the library coffee table. I didn't know much about the New Age. I'd tried to read a book by Shirley MacLaine once, but I hadn't been able to finish it. I had, however, read a number of book reviews of self-proclaimed "classics" in the genre. What those reviews said didn't square with what Cordie was telling me now. Of course, Cordie might be inventing her own brand of New Age religion. A lot of these people did. With Cordie, though, I doubted it. She didn't have that much imagination.

I lit my cigarette with a sterling silver lighter in the shape of Godzilla and said, "Wait a minute. I thought the whole point of channeling was control. You rearrange your psyche or something and—"

Cordie sniffed. "You've been talking to Damon Rask," she said. "He's always been very big on control. But he's a fake, Patience. I knew he was a fake the first time I met him."

"Did you really?" I said.

"Oh, let's not talk about Damon Rask," Elizabeth said. "A man who hanged his own wife, for God's sake. George told us all about it, Patience. I don't know how you meet these people."

"Nobody hanged Delia Grantham," I said automatically. And then, to forestall the questions that leaped instantly into the minds of everyone in the room but Cordie and myself, I turned full face to Cordie and said, *"How* did you know he was a fake?"

Cordie had decided the Tarot readings were over. She was putting the cards back into their box. "I went to his office," she said. "In New York. That was after I'd met him out here, about two years ago. He was having all that trouble with the zoning board, and Katherine Moore had a party for him to see if she could introduce him around and smooth things over. Katherine is a big disciple of his, you know. It was her idea for him to move up here."

"Ah," I said. That explained *that*.

"I liked him a lot when I first met him," Cordie said. "I was very new at all this. I'd been to a couple of seminars in the city, and I'd had a personal session with Jennie Del Mar. That was when I realized I'd been spiritually present at the Harmonic Convergence. You don't know how much better that made me feel. That whole time, while the Harmonic Convergence was going on, I was feeling so *strange*. I thought I was losing my mind. Imagining things. People in the house when I knew I was alone. Voices. Then all of a sudden they stopped, and I didn't know why they'd happened."

"All right," I said. My mind went: *psychotic break*.

Cordie rearranged the afghan around her waist. "I went to his office because of something he said at the party," she said. "He was talking about how much clearer things were in Waverly. Than they were in Greenwich or the City. And I agreed with him. I always felt much more open when I was up here. Much more in touch. As if there was something in the land *speaking* to me. I wasn't getting very far with Jennie then. I wasn't moving forward. I thought I could use a different channeler. Somebody I was more in tune with. So I went to see Damon Rask."

"And?"

Cordie made a little-girl face, disgusted. "He started talking in his voice, the voice of that Egyptian he's supposed to be the channel for, but if he is, he's on the wavelength of a very stupid spirit. The message was all about that gap between the Rask property and the Deverton place. All about how the town put it there to mark the Rask property off as unconsecrated ground, to bury witches in. But Patience, even you must know that isn't true. The only witches ever put to death in Connecticut were hanged in Hartford."

"That's funny," Daddy said. "He didn't say anything about that up here, at least not at the time. He just went on and on about how anybody could have been so stupid as to leave such a useless strip of land."

Chris Bennett snorted. Literally. I'd never seen anybody do that before. "Well, he would say that, wouldn't he?" he said. "I remember him talking about how useless it all was, too, and how worthless. He was just trying to keep the price down. Anybody with any brains could see whoever owned the damn thing was going to get a bundle for it. *If* they kept their heads."

"I thought nobody did own it," Elizabeth said.

"It turns out somebody does," I told her. "It's just that nobody knows who at the moment."

"Well, what would make it valuable, anyway?" Elizabeth said. "It's just a strip. It doesn't cross anything important, at least from what Aunt Louisa says. Who cares?"

"Damon Rask cares," Chris said. "He's an acquisitive man, Elizabeth, and he's an anal compulsive as well. You can see that in his house, all those flat surfaces and nice sharp angles. He wants that land something awful. It's driving him crazy."

"I forgot you spent so much time with Delia and Damon," I said.

Chris shook his head. "I knew this long before I started spending time with them. I met him half a dozen times before Delia did. I could see it right off. Hell, I told Susanna at the time I'd kill to get my hands on that strip. It would pay off my loans and put the down payment on a new office building with no trouble at all."

"I thought you were divorced from Susanna two years ago," I said.

"Getting," Chris said. "It wasn't acrimonious, McKenna. We just drifted along together for a while, and then we drifted apart."

Cordie stirred in her chair, impatient with the way the conversation was going. "You must see what I mean," she said. "He had to be faking that channeling session, and if he was faking that one, he was probably faking all of them. Even if he wasn't, how would I be able to tell? I got out of there as fast as I could. And I never went back, either."

"Did you tell Katherine Moore about the fake?" Uncle Robert was honestly curious.

Cordie was dismissive. "Katherine never had the brains God gave a flea. I told her, but she just said I had to be wrong. If Damon said there were witches in Waverly, there were witches in Waverly."

"It's a piss, isn't it?" Chris said. "The rest of us have to work like dogs, study for years, take responsibility for God knows what, and somebody like Rask comes along, with a talent for voices and an overactive imagination, and the next thing you know he's worth twenty million dollars."

"He's not worth anything like twenty million dollars," Elizabeth said indignantly.

"Oh yes he is," Daddy said. "You forget. I'm on the bank board. He's worth a good deal more than that, and that's just what he admits to. I'd like to be sitting on the IRS auditor's shoulder when they finally decide to do a thorough investigation. And they will."

"Well, I don't see what you're all so surprised about," Cordie said. "There are a lot of silly women out there who'll believe anything anybody tells them, and a lot of those women are rich. What can you expect?"

Even I didn't have an answer to that one—not an answer I could give Cordie, at any rate.

"Maybe I'll go up and change out of these clothes," I said. "I've been in them since six o'clock this morning, and they still feel awful."

"Put on a skirt for once," Elizabeth said automatically. "I don't see why you insist on running around looking like a boy."

I got out of my chair and took another of Mother's courtesy cigarettes. "I hope somebody's doing something about lunch. I haven't eaten all day. And while I'm on that—"

I never got to tell them about that. There was the sound of running footsteps in the hall. Seconds later, Phoebe appeared in the library door, breathless and shining.

"Quick," she said. "In the back room. There's something you've got to see."

EIGHTEEN

THE SOMETHING I HAD TO SEE was a television set, the first I'd ever encountered in a place inhabited by my mother. Even traveling, she had always refused to put up with them. Hotels that provided them automatically were asked to remove them before she arrived. Limousine rental services that equipped their cars with them were not patronized. This set was tucked away in a closetlike room at the back of the house, what I remembered from years ago as "the sewing room." It was, however, state of the art. It had a twenty-six-inch screen. It had a VCR hookup. It had three remotes. It had stereo sound. The shelves that had once held fabric and string had been converted into a slotted tape case and filled with old movies. *Gone with the Wind,* too big to fit into any of the slots, lay on the cabinet's top like a box of gift chocolates.

Elizabeth noticed the anomaly as soon as I did. Like everyone else, she had trailed me down the back hall from the library. Like everyone else, she was now trying to squeeze into the sewing room and find out what was going on. The media equipment stopped her cold. She couldn't have been more surprised if Mother had decided to run off with a gigolo.

"Aunt *Louisa,*" she said. "You bought a *television* set."

On the whole, Mother cared less for televisions than Elizabeth did. She cared less for Elizabeth than she cared for televisions. The tapes were proof she watched very little of what was fed over the tube. She wasn't going to admit that to the woman she had once called "the priggiest five-year-old child in America."

"This is the news, Elizabeth. The local news. If you weren't such a silly little snob, you might learn something."

What this was, actually, was a commercial for Stephen's World of Wheels, a mammoth multibrand car dealership out on Route 6 in Bristol, supposed to be the third largest in the country. Elizabeth refrained from commenting on it. My mother rarely uses language like "silly little snob." Elizabeth knew how to take a hint. She threw herself into a dilapidated overstuffed armchair and waited with the rest of us.

Mother leaned close to my ear and said, "I bought it because of Adrienne, you know. Because she has all those tapes. Then I started to buy tapes myself, and I find they've been a great comfort. A great comfort. You don't know how nice it is to have movies to watch again."

I could just bet. Except for *My Fair Lady,* all of mother's movies seemed to predate both colorization and color.

Stephen's World of Wheels was replaced by the call signal for WTNH-Channel 8, New Haven. A blank map of Connecticut split into bars. The bars spun out to reveal pictures of people I didn't know, but that my mother obviously did. She nodded her head in satisfaction and said, "Good. It's Diane Smith today. She's my favorite one. That other girl must be on vacation." Then, seeming to think this needed explanation, she added, "I like the other girl, too, you understand. And the young man. And I liked Mike Bogaslawski when he was on. But Diane Smith—well. I could have her to the house."

For a bad moment there, I thought Diane Smith was going to be a Litchfield County Lady. She turned out to be an intelligent-looking blonde with a soft-edged but authoritative manner, guilty of neither of the two biggest (and most common) mistakes in female local news anchors. She didn't gush, and she didn't come on so strong you thought she had teeth where more elastic equipment should be. I lit my cigarette and sat back to hear what she had to say.

On the other side of the room, Phoebe bounced up from her perch on the arm of the couch to say, "Shhh." Then a picture flashed on the screen behind Diane Smith's left shoulder, and we all got a look at the Jerry Bauer author photograph of Damon Rask.

"Uh, oh," Chris Bennett said.

"Good afternoon," Diane Smith said. "At the top of the news this hour, police have arrested a Waverly man in what they say may be his second wife murder. Forty-six-year-old Damon Rask was found by a neighbor this morning in the breakfast room of his Brook Hollow Road home. The body of his wife, Cordelia Grantham Rask, a native of Waverly, was found a few feet away, in their greenhouse. She had apparently been hanged.

"Rask gained fame in recent years as a guru of the New Age channeling movement, claiming he was the 'vessel' through which an ancient Egyptian prince, Murhamtep-Ra, could speak to the modern world. His books on Murhamtep-Ra sold in the millions of copies.

"According to police, however, Rask was once someone else—Richard Anderson of Saint Louis, Missouri, a pharmacist and real estate entrepreneur with interests in East Saint Louis, Omaha, and Mission Hills, Kansas. In 1972, Anderson's wife was found dead in their home in the upper-income suburb of Colby, hanging by the neck from a rafter in their living room. Anderson was tried for the crime in early 1973, but was acquitted.

"Police learned of Rask's dual identity during a routine FBI fingerprint check this morning. Rask was under observation at Fairfield Hills Hospital at the time, but he has since been released to a nonpsychiatric facility at St. Mary's Hospital in Waterbury, and the warrant has been served. It's reported that Rask may have been on drugs at the time of the crime.

"In other parts of the state—"

"Other parts of the state," Chris Bennett repeated dazedly. Then he started giggling. "In other parts of the state, for Christ's sake. Who cares what's going on in other parts of the state? Jesus *God.*"

Mother grabbed one of the remotes from the occasional table beside her and shut the set off. She had a thin film of sweat across her forehead, and she looked a little dazed herself.

"I had no idea," she said. "I really had no idea. And to think I had that man in this house for tea, right after he married Delia—"

"I *told* you he was a fake," Cordie said. "No one of true spirituality ever has anything to do with violence. Violence doesn't even touch them. It's not a part of their aura."

"Oh fine," Elizabeth said. "There go the Christian martyrs."

"Don't talk to me about Christian martyrs," Cordie said. "Christianity was the worst thing that ever happened to this planet. Everybody says so, even people who have nothing to do with spirituality. The feminists. The black power people. Christianity—"

"Stop," Mother said. "Stop this nonsensical, blasphemous talk."

"Stop everything," I said. They all looked at me, and I shrugged. "In case you didn't notice, they got at least one fact in that story wrong. Delia didn't die by hanging. And if they got one fact wrong—"

"I don't think you can say that, in this case," Mother said. "I know

Tommy Dick says she didn't die by hanging, and so do you, but it's been reported that she did all morning. If there's been no official word otherwise, I think they were quite within their rights to use it on WTNH. And the rest of that information was— was— well, it must have taken very good reporting, mustn't it?"

"Unless the police released it themselves," I said.

"You're just jealous," Chris Bennett said. "You've got this reputation to maintain as an amateur detective. I think that new information was dynamite, wherever they got it. It explains a hell of a lot of things."

"Like what?" I said.

"Like why Damon Rask was so damned secretive. He kept his papers locked up in a room in the attic, for Christ's sake. Delia hadn't even had a look at their checkbook, and they'd had a joint account since the day they were married. When he had to talk to his lawyer, he went into his office—a soundproofed office, mind you—and locked the door. He must have been scared shitless this was going to come out some day."

"Look," I said, blowing smoke into the air, "I hate to point out the obvious, but he was not exactly a recluse. He had a lot more to worry about getting his face recognized than he did from anything Delia might have overheard when he was talking to his lawyer—*if* you're assuming he was being secretive about his past. He was on every talk show—national, regional, and local—from here to Los Angeles. He had his pictures splashed all over the backs of his books, all over the posters for his books, all over the print ads for his books. Hell, he even did a television ad for one of his books, and he did *lots* of television ads for his seminars."

"All right, then," Chris said, "maybe it explains something else. Maybe it explains why Delia was so frightened all the time. Because she was frightened, Patience. She was scared out of her mind for most of the last six months."

"And you think that was because she was afraid of Damon?"

"What else?" Chris said.

"Well," I said, "for one thing, if she was afraid of Damon, I'd think she'd be more nervous about staying *in* the house than going *out* of it. But if there's one thing everybody has told me about Delia since I've been home, it's that she'd become an agoraphobic. Home was where she wanted to stay, with Damon or without him."

"You're twisting things around," Chris said.

"No, I'm not, Chris. I'm just trying to make sense out of them."

"He killed the last one and he killed her, too," Chris said. "I don't think there's anything else to be said about it."

There was a lot more to be said about it, and everybody was itching to. Nobody did. Chris looked so damn belligerent, and so uncomfortable. His moods could do that, making you suddenly aware of an outsider status you wouldn't have ascribed to him before they started. Elizabeth and Phoebe both started pleating their skirts at once, and Mother got up and started tidying. It was one of those rooms that couldn't be tidied. It needed to be thoroughly cleaned, or left alone.

"I think maybe we ought to go make some lunch now," Mother said. "I'm sure Patience is hungry, and Phoebe is ravenous, and I know I could use a little soup. It's been so very cold the last couple of days."

"Soup," Elizabeth said, in approximately the tone of voice used by Saint Thomas to proclaim "my Lord and my God." "I hadn't thought of soup. I would love soup."

"We could make some of those little sandwiches, too," Mother said. "The ones with the melted cheese on them. George ought to be back with the almonds any minute now. He loves those sandwiches."

"All men love those sandwiches," Elizabeth said, as if she knew.

Sometime in the middle of the argument—or maybe the middle of the news broadcast—I had wrestled myself out of my boots and folded my legs up under me. Now I got my legs unwound and my boots picked up off the floor, and stubbed my cigarette into the only ashtray.

"I'm going to go up and change first," I said. "These damn things are cutting off all the circulation in my legs. I must be getting fat."

"You're not getting fat," Phoebe said.

"Whatever. I think I'll just—"

The phone went off somewhere close, and I jumped. Mother never allowed a lot of phones in the house. She never permitted them in the bedrooms, because people should not be awakened by importunate callers. She never permitted them in the main living room, either, because people shouldn't make or receive phone calls while entertaining or being entertained—and that's what living rooms were *for*. It made me wonder how much time she spent in her television room.

The ringing went on and on, and finally mother said, "Patience. It's right there. Practically under your hand."

I looked down and saw a plain, old-fashioned black instrument, the kind that had to be installed by a forty-dollar-an-hour service person. I picked up the receiver.

"Hello?" I said.

"Hello yourself," Tommy Dick said. "I thought I'd catch you. How're you doing?"

"I'm doing fine," I told him. "But I think you're full of it."

"You saw the news?"

"Diane Smith on Channel 8."

"Yeah," Tommy said. "Your mother always watches Diane Smith if she's on. Big fan. But I'm not full of it, Pay. We discovered a few things after you left this morning."

"Like what?"

"Like rope burns on his hands. He strung her up, McKenna. He got that rope out of the greenhouse toolbox and he wrapped it around her neck and he threw it over a rafter and he strung her up. No question whatsoever."

"She didn't die from hanging, Tommy."

"I know that. I also know there's no question about the match on those fingerprints. None whatsoever. The guy really is Richard Anderson and he probably killed his first wife. He's a pill head and a nut. And—"

"What kind of pill head?" I said.

"Valium. That's what they found in him at the hospital, and that's what we're going to find in that health drink of his when we get it analyzed. He's down off it now, you know. Just as sane as you and me. *And* closeted with his lawyer. But he strung her up, McKenna. And we're going to get him."

"Fine," I said. "Now answer me one more question. What about my Great-Aunt Felicia?"

"We'll know by the end of the week."

"That's it?"

"That's it."

"You're out of your gourd," I said.

There was a lot of coughing and hacking on the line. Tommy must have lost his battle with Demon Tobacco again, just as I had mine.

"Listen to me," he said.

"I've been listening to you," I said.

"Then trust me."

"I do. I just don't trust your logic."

"My logic is fine. It's the only possible answer. It's the *best* possible answer. Think about it for a minute and you'll know that, too."

"Tommy—"

"I've got to get off. Rask's lawyer is some hotshot from New York with a contract firm with connections in Hartford. The prosecutor's office is on my ass."

"Tommy," I said again. No good. The phone had gone to dial tone in my hand.

I put it back in the cradle and looked up to find my mother frowning at me.

"Tommy Dick?" she said.

"Exactly," I said.

"Well," she said. "Patience, I know how you are when you feel strongly about things. I know that. You were the same way at two months old when you wanted to be carried in my *left* arm and not my *right*. But this is Tommy's job. He is supposed to be expert at it. And husbands do most often kill wives."

I shook my head at her. The rest of them were all still there, looking at me. I didn't want to get into an elaborate argument with the peanut gallery looking on. Maybe I didn't want to get into an argument at all. Aside from objections, and I had hundreds of those, I didn't have much to say.

"Let me go get changed," I said. "You go make soup and I'll come down and eat it all."

That broke the mood, finally. Mother smiled happily and went shooing the others out into the hall, clucking about Vitamin C and Vitamin D and how *careful* you had to be about your health in bad weather. She made a big point of letting them know she wasn't wedded to the old argument about how rain caused colds. It was lack of sunlight she was worried about.

I stood in the middle of the floor and checked out the tapes for the second time, feeling oddly depressed. Then, because I felt guilty about not moving, I moved. I went down the back hall to the back stairs and then up to the second floor, wishing for the first time on this trip that I had Nick with me.

Nick has good points and bad, but his very best point is his willingness to listen to me. For hours. Without interruption. No matter how little sense or how little headway I'm making.

One thing Nicholas George Carras never does is leave me with a head full of questions and nobody to work them out with.

NINETEEN

I GOT CHANGED RIGHT AWAY—into regular jeans and a fresh shirt and a dry sweater and a pair of those L.L. Bean ankle boots that feel like slippers—and all the time I was doing it I was in a hurry. That happens to me sometimes when I'm depressed. Instead of sinking into sloth and inertia, I become convinced there's something urgent I have to do, if I can just get through these nitpicking little details I've procrastinated about so long. I took my hair out of its braid and went at it with a brush for a hundred whacking strokes. When I was done, the skin of my scalp was prickly and hot. I braided my hair up again and twisted it into a knot at the top of my spine. I put on a pair of sterling silver shell earrings Nick had given me for my last birthday. I even buffed up my engagement ring. I forget about my engagement ring, most of the time. It was Nick's mother's idea, not his or mine. It's too big and too bright. Sometimes when I'm alone at night on the street in the city, it makes me afraid for my life.

When I got all this done, I stopped dead in the middle of my room and realized there was nothing left to do—except go down for lunch. Nice thought, that. I could just see them, sitting around the kitchen table, trying to be bitchy without letting my mother know about it. I got a pack of cigarettes from the carton in my suitcase and sat down on my bed to light up. I wanted to eat, but I didn't want to eat with the rest of them. I wanted to rest, but not while I had all these questions. I wanted to wring Tommy Dick's neck. I wanted a lot of things.

After a while, this began to feel stupid. I put out my cigarette and got off the bed, determined to go downstairs and force myself through another McKenna family therapy session. Then I went out in the hall, looked around, and decided to give myself the pettiest sort of reprieve. I might have to go downstairs. I didn't have to do it in a hurry.

The bedroom wings extend to each side of the core building and are connected to the foyer by staircases that end at either side of the front door. They're also connected to the back hall by staircases.

They're also connected to each other, by a balcony walk that crosses over the main living room. In my grandmother's day, this walk was open. Anyone in the living room could see anyone on the walk, and vice versa. One of the first things my mother did when she took over the house was to have this walk curtained. The point of it was to allow people to cross from bedroom to bedroom without having to pass through the common rooms of the house. People who wanted to do that almost always wanted to do it in bedclothes.

To get to the balcony walk, I had to go all the way to the back of the family bedroom wing, down a short hall, and through a pair of connecting doors. Then I had to be quiet. I couldn't be seen, but I might be heard. The last thing I wanted was a lot of questions about what I was doing "prowling around" upstairs—"prowling around" being the way Elizabeth would put it, if she caught me. I practically inched my way to the other side of the house. Below me, the living room was silent. I didn't trust it. Sometimes I think the McKenna family motto is: *sneak first, think up a reason for it later.*

There was another pair of connecting doors on the guest bedroom side, and another short hall. I went through both of these and came out in the bedroom hall proper. It was longer and wider than the hall assigned to us. It had many more bedrooms, and a couple of staid, claustrophobic suites. Mother always put the Gold Coast relatives in the guest wing. She always put Phoebe in with the family. The woman has a great deal of character.

I went down the hall slowly, looking into rooms whose doors were open, meaning most of them. Cordie had a stack of books by the side of her bed that was almost as tall as she was. The one on top had a pyramid on the dust jacket, and the pyramid had eyes. Robert had a collection of Civil War soldiers on his bureau. They'd been given to him by his father, and he brought them with him wherever he went, even to hotels. Elizabeth had a brown-tinted photograph of our great-grandmother lying on the pillows of her bed.

The door just past Elizabeth's was wide open, propped back with a rubber stopper. The windows were open, too. I stopped and looked inside. The bed had been made. The floor had been swept. The rug had been vacuumed. Beyond that, I didn't think my mother would have done anything to the place. If the room was barren and empty, it was because Felicia had wanted it barren and empty.

Felicia.

I stepped back, then stepped forward again. At second glance, the room wasn't quite as barren as it had seemed. It was just neat to the point of insanity. Like Cordie, Felicia had books. Unlike Cordie, she had put them away on the built-in shelves under the windows. I crossed the room and checked them out. *First Families of New England,* one said, and *The Connecticut Yankee Register.* I checked the publishers' logos and found what I expected. Most of the books had been privately published, by the kind of women's "historical" society that serves more as a social imprimatur than an educational organization.

I got up and looked around again. There was a silver pillbox, a silver pen, and a small leather-covered notebook on the night table. I checked them out. The pillbox was empty. The leather notebook had writing on only the first page, and that just said: *Auchincloss. Vanderbilt Era.* A book. I went back to the bookcase and found it. Then I went back to the notebook.

"Weird," I said, out loud. I looked into the wastebasket, but it had been emptied. Someday I'm going to have to convince my mother that there are drawbacks to being conscientiously clean.

I went to the wardrobe and opened it. There was nothing in there but skirts on skirt hangers and shoes on shoe trees. I went to the bureau and opened the first two drawers, but that was just underwear.

In the third drawer, I got a little luckier. That held a large, square satin-quilted box. It was the kind of thing women used to keep sewing kits in, in the days when doing embroidery was a mark of being a lady, and no lady ever left her hands idle. I opened it and found a little cascade of invitations—to weddings, to parties, to dances, to receptions. Felicia didn't seem to have kept invitations to charity balls— maybe because those could be bought. She had kept invitations to college graduations, if the young woman graduating had been prominent enough. She had one for a Lee King Van Rensselaer, at Smith. She did not have mine.

At the bottom of the box, there was a little stack of invitations bound with a rubber band. If they'd looked older, I would have ignored them, expecting them to be from her debutante year. Nothing in the box was that old, but it seemed like the kind of thing Felicia would keep. And drag around with her. Since the envelopes were fresh and not discolored at all, I opened them.

They turned out to be a series of invitations to the annual dinner dance of the Connecticut branch of the Colonial Dames of America.

Year after year, from 1964 until just a few months ago, the Colonial Dames had fed themselves in a body during the third week of October. They'd always fed themselves at the same place—the Red Haddock Inn—and they'd always fed themselves the same things. Pumpkin chicken. Indian pudding. Oyster stew. Just reading about it made me feel stuffed. I tried to visualize the place, and came up with the picture of a large, white colonnaded building out on the Deerfield Run, out where—

Out where the old Marsh place used to be, before Will had died and Willie had taken up residence in my mother's stable office.

I paged through the invitations and found the one for 1988. October twenty-first, seven o'clock. When had old Will died, exactly? I didn't think anyone had ever told me. They'd just said he'd died on the Deverton place, and it had been a while before Willie found him.

"Funny," I said, out loud again.

"I don't see anything funny about it," Elizabeth said. "Sneaking through people's things when they're dead and can't defend themselves."

I turned and found her standing in the doorway. She had her arms folded over her chest, in conscious imitation of my mother. It wasn't working. She'd always been afraid of me. Resentful, too, and hostile—but always afraid. She never knew what to expect from me.

I put the Colonial Dames' invitations back in their rubber band and dumped them in the box.

"I didn't mean funny ha-ha," I said, "I meant funny weird. I got all the times completely mixed up."

"What times, Patience?"

"The times in 1988," I said. "People kept telling me things about old Will dying, and Damon marrying Delia, and Chris and Susanna getting a divorce, and I kept thinking they'd happened over the course of two years. But they hadn't. They all happened at just about the same time."

"Well, of course they did," Elizabeth said. "I don't see how that excuses you from rummaging through Felicia's things."

"I'm not looking for an excuse for rummaging through her things. Go tell Mother. I don't care. Do you remember any of this stuff? Were you here at the time?"

Elizabeth shrugged. "I was at that dinner you were looking at the invitation to. Felicia always made me come. And I knew about the divorce, and about Delia Grantham and Damon Rask, or whoever he is. Everybody did."

"I didn't."

"You were in New York." Elizabeth sniffed. I'd been in the *wrong part* of New York. "Your friend Delia brought Damon Rask to that dinner, even though she wasn't married to him yet. And Susanna brought Chris Bennett, even though they'd already filed for divorce. The old ladies nearly died."

"Susanna and Chris had just filed? They weren't actually divorced yet?"

"They weren't divorced for ages. Honestly, Patience, I think your Dr. Bennett is a gigolo. All that public fighting over money. And Damon Rask—"

"Yes?"

"Well, everybody knew what he was doing there, and everybody knew what he was doing marrying Delia. He just wanted an in with the right people. And he got it, of course. People like him always do."

"What about the surveying?" I said. "Was that going on then?"

"It had been finished a few months before. They were looking at the provenance of the strip, I think. What I heard was that nobody expected anybody to own it, and Damon Rask was going to buy it as soon as the investigation was done. I don't know why he hasn't bought it yet."

"The investigation got a little complicated," I said. "What about Willie Marsh? Was he at this dinner?"

"Of course not. The Colonial Dames is a women's organization, Patience. Jedra Marsh died years ago, and Willie isn't married. Besides, she probably couldn't have gotten in anyway. The Marshes are—"

"White trash" isn't a New England expression, but it was the one Elizabeth wanted to use. If we got into a fight about that, it would last a week.

"What about Cordie?" I asked her. "What about Mother? What about Daddy and Uncle Robert?"

"Your parents weren't there," Elizabeth said. "Aunt Louisa never goes. She—well, she's quite unreasonably prejudiced against that sort of thing. Sometimes I thought she only did it to annoy Great-Aunt Felicia. Uncle Robert and Cordie came."

"Did Felicia make them, too?"

"Felicia wasn't a monster, Patience."

Yes, she was—but I didn't want to get into an argument about that, either. I shoved the box back into the drawer and stood up. Half an hour ago, I had been dragging around, exhausted and without direction. Now I had a million ideas, and Elizabeth in the way of following through on any of them. I tried to think of a way to end the conversation politely, and couldn't do it.

I looked around the room, and found the notebook again.

"Elizabeth," I said, "did you buy a Louis Auchincloss book for Felicia the day she died?"

"I never bought books for Felicia. Felicia bought her own books."

"What about her notebook? I looked in it and it was practically empty—"

"You *looked* in it?"

"It wasn't locked with a key, Elizabeth. It's just a plain open notebook with one line of writing in it. Title and author. The Auchincloss book."

Elizabeth sighed. "I don't know what business this is of yours, Patience, but every morning Felicia wrote down what she had to do that day, and every night she tore the page off. She'd been doing it like that for years. She was taught to at Farmington, in the days when Farmington *was* Farmington."

"So if there's a title and author there, she wanted to buy that book? And if she has that book, then she bought it the same day, the day she died?"

"I suppose so."

"Did she go out that day? The impression I got is that she spent the whole morning sitting in that chair, glaring at people."

"Felicia did not glare. And I haven't the faintest idea whether she went out or not. I wasn't here the whole time myself."

"Were you gone long?"

"Long enough to catch my breath. Really, Patience, I know you think you're some kind of detective, but—"

"Never mind," I said. I gave the room one last look and then made an end run around Elizabeth, right out the door. "Tell Mother I won't be down for lunch, will you? I'll be back in a couple of hours."

"But Patience, Aunt Louisa—"

"Just *tell* her," I said.

I went out into the hall and down the back way again, although I wasn't headed for the balcony this time. I was on my way to the back stairs. At the bottom of them was an outside door. On the other side of that door was the back of the garages. I was in such a hurry, I didn't even worry about driving the Jeep.

Elizabeth, having no sense of proportion, followed me all the way to the top of the steps, complaining.

"You're so thoughtless," she kept saying. "Aunt Louisa is down in the kitchen right this minute, making soup just because you said you wanted it, and she's not been brought up to it, you know, she's only doing it because she loves you, and here you are—"

Natter, natter, natter. Something in my brain caught the rhythm of it and wouldn't let it go. I had that voice in my head all the way down the drive and out onto the Old Canfield Road.

TWENTY

I GOT TO WATERBURY right in the middle of the after-lunch rush, and because I was unfamiliar with the streets, I got lost. For a while, I went around and around the town common, looking for the main post office. I was sure it would be there. I hadn't been to Waterbury often, but I'd been there under the best circumstances for remembering where things were. In 1982, my father had had a gall bladder operation. He'd been in St. Mary's Hospital, where Damon Rask was supposed to be now, for twelve days. On every one of those days, I'd gone up to visit him. I'd even driven myself. I thought I'd be able to find the place with no problem at all.

Instead, I went around and around the traffic circle, seeing nothing that looked familiar. Neat, orderly lines of working people lined up for the bus—mostly official-looking black ladies in good linen suits and professional heels. Less-neat teenagers hung out around the War Memorial, looking cold. A man with an American flag in his lapel and a Budweiser bottle in a brown paper bag in his pocket paced back and forth in front of the walk light, never crossing the street. I cursed the changing traffic lights and the left-turn-only lanes and went around in a circle once again.

Finally, I got myself off the treadmill and up the hill beyond the green. Traffic was a little lighter there, and I was able to pull over to the curb. I flagged down a boy carrying an armload of pizza boxes and asked him where the hospital was.

He looked at me like I'd just arrived from Venus and said, "Next light. Turn right. It's right *there.*"

Of course it was. I wasn't even on the right road.

I got the Jeep started again and went. A few minutes later, it *was* right there, a square reddish building with a concrete-shaded parking lot attached to it. The parking lot had signs that said EMERGENCY VISITORS plastered all over it, but I pulled in anyway. I'd wasted enough time going around in circles. The regular visitors' lot could be anywhere. I'd probably never find it. Fortunately, the emergency lot was empty. I didn't have to feel guilty about taking up ambulance space.

Of course, as soon as I got inside, there'd be an emergency of world-class proportions, involving three city buses and a propane truck. I'd hear my license plate number on the loudspeaker and have to move.

Except that I didn't know my license plate number.

I went through the automatic doors and asked at emergency admitting for the information desk. It was down several hallways, up several elevators, and next to the gift shop. I took off, feeling as if I were disintegrating. Literally.

By the time I got to the information desk, I was a mess—my hair coming out of its braid, my shirt coming out of my jeans. I tucked myself in as well as I could, under the watchful eyes of a nun in mufti who probably thought she couldn't be recognized as a nun. They always think that. I can always spot them at two hundred yards.

The woman at the information desk, not being a nun, just gave me the once-over and a little "tsk-tsk." Then she asked if she could help me.

"I've come to see Damon Rask," I told her. "I am—was—a friend of his wife's."

It's always a bad idea to underestimate the intelligence of middle-aged ladies. This one went from fluffy to shrewd in two seconds flat. She looked me over one more time, and she didn't like what she saw.

"You don't look like a reporter," she said.

"I'm not a reporter," I said. "My name is Patience Campbell McKenna. I'm a friend."

"A friend," she said. "Mr. Rask didn't say anything about friends."

"I can't help that," I said.

"The *police* didn't say anything about friends."

"Has Mr. Rask got a police guard?"

She bit her lip, shook her head, and picked up her phone. I didn't like the way this was going. I'd forgotten all about the police—all about everything, except that there was a question I had to ask Damon Rask. If Rask did have a police guard, and that guard was Tommy Dick, I'd be in. If he didn't, or if the man on duty was somebody I didn't know, I was dead. I racked my brains for anything I might ever have heard about St. Mary's Hospital. It was a small place. The big facility was across town, at Waterbury General. And Kathy, my brother's George's wife, had worked at St. Mary's before her marriage. She was, after all, a nurse.

Sacred Heart Three.

The words popped into my head from nowhere at all. Once there, they refused to be dislodged. Sacred Heart Three was a floor of private rooms in the most newly renovated part of the hospital. Kathy had worked there for three months before she got pregnant with Andrea, her first. It was a mixed ward, medically and sexually. There were women there recovering from drug overdoses and men recovering from prostate cancer. It was the place you went if you could afford to be comfortable as well as cared for.

It was also a long shot, but less long than the hope that I'd be able to get anywhere with the lady at the information desk. She was still talking into her phone. She was getting more animated by the minute. Her animation was not happy. In fact, I was beginning to think she loathed me.

I waited until she turned her head away from me again—she did this every other minute—and then took off back toward the elevators. I found "Sacred Heart Three" on the information board, and pushed the call button for "up." The elevator doors opened to dislodge a little clutch of white-coated lab technicians, all complaining about the price of uniform shoes.

I got in after they got out, pushed "3," and went up. I got off as soon as the doors opened. In front of me, a sign was bolted to the wall reading, "Visiting Hours. 8 A.M. to 8 P.M." I looked down the long, wide hallway to the nurses' station. There was nobody there but one clerk, typing away at something in quadruplicate.

I walked down to the station and turned onto the hall proper. There were nurses there, bringing things to and from rooms, but none of them was interested in me. I passed a little kitchen and a door that said "Dietician." Then I looked in on a couple of patients. They both had their lunches on bed trays, and they both looked disgruntled.

I had expected to find a police presence of some kind. Not seeing one, I began to think I was in the wrong place. Damon Rask was under arrest for murder. Even if he was already out on bail—not impossible, if his lawyer's connections were good enough—there ought to be *some* indication that he wasn't a regular patient. At least, I thought there ought to be.

I checked in on a couple of more patients, and then I came to a room with the door closed. It was the only door on the floor that *was* closed. I didn't think that meant the room was empty. In that case, it would make more sense to keep the door all the way open. It might mean the patient inside was smoking his head off. That's what I'd do if I was ever confined to a hospital.

I wanted to be smoking even now.

I looked up the long hall for signs of nosy nurses and found none. Then I took a deep break and pushed the door lever. If whoever was in that room wasn't Damon Rask, and didn't want to see me, I was going to get myself thrown out on my ass.

Fortunately for me, the patient in that room was Damon Rask. Not so fortunately, he wasn't anywhere near as doped up as he'd been the last time I'd seen him. When I appeared in the doorway he looked up, sat up, and said,

"Just *who* the *hell* are you?"

I told him. "My name's Pay McKenna," I said. "I was the woman who walked in on you this morning. I came to find out if you had a nervous breakdown after your first wife died."

Damon Rask's eyes nearly bugged out of his head.

And then he burst out laughing.

After that, it was all right—or as all right as it could ever be with Damon Rask, who was just as strange as I remembered him from the city. He made me go back and close the door. When I'd done that and reestablished myself in his visitor's chair, he reached into the drawer of his utility table and came up with a bottle of champagne.

"Not exactly appropriate, maybe, but the best I can do. It was all I could get hold of."

"Are you allowed to drink that stuff in here?" I asked him.

"Nope," he said. "And I'm especially not supposed to drink it because they gave me some speed to wear the Valium off. Or whatever it was. On the other hand—"

"There's nothing I can do to stop you," I said.

"Exactly." He eased the cork off—the bottle had been opened once already; it was simpler than it might have been—and poured champagne into a couple of clear plastic water glasses. "You're very smart, you know," he said. "Nobody else even thought of asking that question. And it is the question, isn't it?"

"You haven't answered it."

"No, I haven't. Smoke, if you want. From what I understand, it's allowed in the rooms. If it isn't, it's just too bad. I've been doing it all day."

I got my cigarettes out, but I didn't light up. It didn't feel right. *"Did* you have a nervous breakdown?" I asked him.

"I spent four months in a psychiatric facility in Saint Louis. With acute depression. The police thought I was faking."

"Were you?"

"No."

"And did you kill her?"

"No to that, too. Marian was a pain in the ass, but I wouldn't have had to kill her to get rid of her. The divorce laws aren't that rough these days." He swigged three quarters of his champagne and refilled his glass. "They finally decided she did it to herself, you know."

"Did you love Delia?"

He smiled slightly. "I was happy with Delia. I don't think I fall in love the way people say they do. I liked having Delia around. I liked what she was—except for the agoraphobia, and we were taking care of that. I've never understood people who jump from one wife to the next. What for?"

"Youth," I said. "Beauty. Money."

"Ah yes. The grand old self-delusion. Death won't happen if you just stay away from people who are dying. But we're all dying."

"That," I said, "is the kind of thing you say in your books."

"And my books are what you think I'm faking."

"Aren't you?"

"Oh, definitely. And faking them well, too, if I must say so myself. Delia didn't know that, in case you're wondering. And it doesn't matter that you do. It's just your word against mine. Unless you're wired. Are you wired?"

"No."

"That's good. Let me tell you something about the United States of America, Miss McKenna. If you want to get rich here, you don't *make* anything. The tax laws will kill you. You provide a service. The tax laws are very good to you there. And the best possible service to provide is religion. The churches are such a mess, nobody knows what the word means any more, and everybody is looking for spirituality without cost. Provide religion. Junk politics and morality."

"Marvelous," I said.

"Don't blame me," Damon Rask said. "I wasn't the one who talked the World Council of Churches into taking a stand on American intervention in Central America. I wasn't the idiot who convinced the rest of the idiots that sex was more important than food, either."

"Somehow, I expected to see you more broken up," I said. "You were—very out of it this morning. On another planet, as my niece would say. I thought you'd be distraught."

"Because you thought that had happened because of my feelings for Delia?" Rask nodded. "Yes, I can see that. But it wasn't that. It was—well, for one thing, I was stoked to the gills on some kind of downers. Which I didn't take myself, no matter what the police think. They're checking into my morning milkshake. By the time I came downstairs and found her, I was flying. And then—"

"Then?"

"There she was, lying on the floor of the greenhouse. Just as dead as Marian had been. And I—"

"Do you remember stringing her up?"

"No," he said, "but I'm not going to deny I did that. Look at my hands." He held them out, welted and raw. "Obviously, I must have done that. The last time, I cut her down—cut Marian down—and got her dressed up in a nightgown and put her to bed. That's how I ended up being arrested. I messed all the evidence up. And I can't remember doing that, either. When I came out of it, they asked me what I'd done, and all I could think of was—nothing."

"You ought to get that checked into," I said.

"I've had it checked into, Miss McKenna. I've seen more psychiatrists than I knew existed before Marian was dead. They aren't telling me what I want to hear."

I got out of the chair and went to the window. Through it, I could see St. Mary's School, run by an order of nuns that had never heard of "modern" habits. Their veils fluttered in the wind, black and wide as capes.

"Tell me a few other things," I said, "just to satisfy my curiosity."

"What other things?"

"Two years ago, around the time you were getting engaged to Delia, she took you to a dinner party for the Colonial Dames. It was held at a place called the Red Haddock Inn. Do you remember that?"

"Vaguely. She took me to a lot of things like that. She was very dedicated to social history."

"A couple of months before that dinner, you'd had your land surveyed. That was when they found that strip. Do you remember what was happening with that at the time? Did you still think the town owned it? Had you offered to buy it?"

"I offered to buy it right away," Rask said. "As soon as I knew it was there. I don't think we had any idea whether somebody owned it or not, then."

"When did you know?"

He thought about it. "That's hard to say. I hired a lawyer to do a title search almost immediately, and then things went back and forth for a while. I remember we couldn't just do the ordinary things. The situation was too unusual. But we did do the ordinary things first. That was when we found out there wasn't any ordinary title to the place, nothing registered. Right after that, I made an offer to the town, in case it turned out they owned it. And then things got held up a little."

"Held up how?"

Rask shrugged. "I had a book tour coming up. I was gone on and off for about six months. One of the agencies I had looking into it, the Office of Historical Districts, was closed for a while. They were doing renovations and their records were in a mess. We had to wait for that. Then we found out that there might be someone with title, someone living, that is, and we had to turn the whole thing over to the genealogy people. That's where it was last time I checked. This Hendershot guy had about eight million great-grandchildren. They were tracing down every one of them and coming up blank. So far. With that many descendants, though, you have to assume you're going to find somebody."

"So for the past two years, you've just been blithering around about this? You haven't made it a priority?"

"It's not a question of life and death, Miss McKenna. It's just an annoyance. And a matter of pride, I guess. *Somebody's* going to buy that strip. It might as well be me."

"You're going to stay on in Waverly?"

"I'd better. I've built myself a highly expensive and highly unmarketable house."

I came back to the chair, laughing. "You're right," I said. "If I was looking for a place to live, I'd take one look at that flying saucer of yours and relocate to Florida."

"Don't knock it. It plays in Peoria."

"One more thing?" I said. "Going to that Colonial Dames dinner, whose idea was it, yours or Delia's?"

"Neither. Chris Bennett talked Delia into it. He said his soon-to-be-ex was insisting, and he didn't want to go alone."

"Ah," I said.

"More champagne?" he said.

"Sorry. I've got to get out of here. Got to see a man about a stake."

He shrugged and topped up his own glass. "You know," he said, "I wouldn't be too judgmental, if I were you. About me, I mean. Sociopathology can be a virtue, really. If you use it right."

I let that one pass. I had to.

TWENTY-ONE

THERE WAS A PILEUP on Route 69—that was why I was so late getting home. It was truck day on the Interstate. I got off because I don't like being surrounded by eighteen-wheelers, and because I thought it would be faster. I was barely a quarter of a mile off the highway when I had to stop. A green Toyota and a Cadillac Coupe de Ville had gone head to head on the center line. Cars coming around the curves from both directions had plowed into their sides. By the time I got there, the landscape was littered with police cars and ambulances, and cars were stopped for miles. More cars came and stopped behind me, wedging me in. I wasn't going anywhere until the authorities told me I could.

I spent a few minutes beeping my horn and swearing at imaginary enemies, and then I relaxed. There are drivers who can go on that way for hours. I'm not one of them. I don't see what good it does, and honking horns give me a headache. I put the Jeep into park and got a pad of paper and a pen out of the glove compartment. I already had my cigarettes out. This always happens to me when I think I've begun to figure something out. I get agitated, crazy, sure I have to go out and *do* something, right this minute. It wears off after a while, if I let it. On at least two occasions, I have not let it. Both those times, I have nearly gotten myself killed.

At the top of the first piece of paper on the pad, I wrote a name. It was a name I was sure of, because it was the only one I could match up with motive, opportunity, and suspicious behavior. Especially suspicious behavior. I couldn't believe I'd been lied to so often and so cavalierly—and so *inconsistently.* That was the hard thing to take. If you're going to lie, you ought at least to remember what you said. This person hadn't, and hadn't seemed to care. What was worse, I'd barely noticed.

I drew a line under the name and held the pen ready to write, then stopped. What did I know, exactly? What did I know that I could prove?

For one thing, I knew the whole thing had started with that strip of land and the death of Old Will Marsh. My murderer had known before anyone else that that strip had a traceable title and who that title belonged to. My murderer had also had reasons, desperate reasons, to keep that information from coming out in the summer and fall of 1988.

But Old Will Marsh must have had that information, too, or been close to getting it. Everyone said he was a fanatic about the Deverton place. He had researched it and researched it. What he hadn't read about, he had probably talked about. There were half a dozen very old people in town who knew bits and pieces of things. Will would have brought those things together, mulled over them, worked them like a jigsaw. When the strip was discovered, he would have gone to work on that. I'd have to ask Willie to be sure, but it seemed inevitable.

So my murderer had known, and Old Will Marsh had known—and Old Will Marsh had had to die, because he couldn't have been shut up. Fanatics usually can't.

After that, things got speculative. I believed them because I had to. I didn't have evidence I could hand over to Tommy Dick. The official reading on Old Will's death was that he had had a heart attack, fallen down a well and died. If my theory was correct, whatever had given him that heart attack had to have been administered well beforehand, and not at the Deverton place. There was only one reason I could think of for my murderer to have killed Felicia McKenna and Delia Grantham Rask. They must have seen that murder being committed, without *knowing* they were seeing it. And something must have happened—or be about to happen—that would make that very clear.

Whatever had killed Old Will Marsh must have been given to him on the night of October twenty-first, 1988, before, during or after the dinner the Colonial Dames gave at the Red Haddock Inn. That's the only time they'd all been together. It was also one of the few occasions on which they were likely to be.

But what had happened recently that would set the whole thing going again? Something that revealed who owned that strip of land, obviously. That would provide motive where none had been before. What might have seemed like an accident or a mistake at the time would now look deliberate. But what could have happened?

The town wasn't on the verge of closing its investigation and declaring an owner. Cassie and Ellen at the Office of Historical Districts had been clear about that.

I knew a reasonable amount about my murderer's financial condition. There was nothing to indicate there had been any recent change, any impetus for sudden revelations.

Not a damn thing was going on in town that didn't go on every day, except for my wedding. I was *sure* that had nothing to do with this.

Behind me, the driver of a canary yellow Honda lost it. He put his elbow on his horn and *leaned.* It made my head feel ready to split apart.

I threw the pad and pen back into the glove compartment and went for my cigarettes. I had now been caught in the aftermath of the pileup for three quarters of an hour. Nothing I could see indicated that I was about to be released.

The ambulances and police cars were still blocking both sides of the road.

The wreckers had arrived to make it worse.

I didn't know what had killed Will Marsh, or Felicia and Delia.

Or what had happened on the night of the Colonial Dames' dinner.

Or what had happened, over the last few days or weeks, to make this mess inevitable.

The way the cleanup was going up ahead, I was beginning to think I was never going to know.

By the time I got home it was early dark, and the turnaround in front of our garages was so full of cars, I couldn't get the Jeep into it. The tarp on Uncle Robert's tank had been dusted of snow and the loose flap refastened. Elizabeth's BMW sat under piles of white and looked neglected. The rest of the vehicles looked hot, as if they'd only recently arrived. George's Land Rover, Chris's Porsche, Susanna's Volvo, even Tommy Dick's police car. There had to be a convention going on in there.

I parked in the drive in front of the porch and thought about going in through the foyer, but I wasn't ready for that. If they were all there together, they were fighting. Either that, or the Pope wasn't Polish after all. I got out and went around back, toward the kitchen door. The path to that part of the house was the single cleanest piece of land in Waverly, Connecticut. My mother knows what's important. Her relatives can break their necks on icy pavements. Her housekeeper has to be protected.

I let myself in the back door, took off my boots, and threw them into the closet across from the pantry. There were sounds coming from the kitchen, banging crockery and *pinging* metal, as if somebody who wasn't used to it was making tea. I peeked in, just in case whoever it was was somebody I didn't want to see. It turned out to be young Will Marsh, trying to read the directions on the back of a box of Tetley.

I let myself into the kitchen and said, "Hi. I'll do that if you want me to."

He must have heard me in the vestibule. He didn't jump. "Hi yourself," he said. "And please do it. Your friend Phoebe is feeling faint."

"Oh dear," I said.

"I don't know much about being pregnant, Patience, but I think we're going to have a little problem here. Maybe about seven pounds six ounces."

"Maybe we'll have to cancel the wedding."

He shook his head and handed me the tea box. I took it. "I never knew anybody wanted to get married so bad and wanted to have a wedding so little. You're a pip, McKenna."

"I'm a sane woman," I said. The kettle was light, so I took it to the tap and filled it all the way up. People being people, as soon as Phoebe got her tea, five others were going to want some. I put the kettle on the stove and turned the gas on under it, then went looking through cupboards for a big enough pot.

"So," I said, "what's going on in there? Do I want to know? Does anybody? Why is the entire town of Waverly in my mother's living room?"

"Tommy Dick is doing an Ellery Queen."

"An Ellery Queen?"

"He has all the suspects in one room—or all the people who could reasonably be suspects in a bad detective novel—and he's giving them chapter and verse about how Damon Rask killed Delia Grantham."

"Damon Rask didn't kill Delia Grantham," I said.

"You keep saying that. I keep listening to Tommy Dick. Who else would have killed her, McKenna? I know I'm supposed to swallow Dad's death as an accident. I know it's never going to be proved to be anything else. But it wasn't an accident. He may have been seventy-six, but he'd never had a heart condition in his life. I can't think of a single person who'd want to kill him but Rask."

"You mean you can't think of a single person you'd want to be the one who'd killed him. Will, that's different."

"Not really. Rask was a bastard, all the way down the line. I think he was the only person in town who was ever anything but good to Dad. Shit, McKenna. They took care of him. Everybody did. If I had to be away, they went out to the house and made sure he ate, they—"

"Stop," I said.

"Stop what?"

"Were you away just before he died? Were you away on October twenty-first?"

"1988?"

"Of course 1988."

"How the hell am I supposed to know? That was—"

"Think," I said. "Think hard."

"Crap." I had taken down a pile of tea mugs. Will took them out of my hands. "How the hell do you think I'm supposed to be able to remember after all this time—it would be different if you were talking about the day I found him, I'd remember that, I—wait."

"Yes?"

"You know, I think I might have been. Away, I mean. That was the year—they have these shows every year in Hartford, custom furniture, carpentry, detail work, that kind of thing. Like boat shows and car shows, you know. Where people who work with stuff and people who sell stuff get together to check out what's new. They hold it in November, usually, but that year there was trouble getting the Civic Center for the right time. Some rock group on tour, I think. Anyway, it was moved up. It might have been that weekend."

"If it had been that weekend, somebody would have gone out and made sure your father ate dinner?"

"Absolutely."

"Fine," I said. "That takes care of that. Now, if I just knew a couple of other things."

"Take the kettle off," Will said. "It's boiling over."

It was and I did. I dumped a load of tea bags into the pot and poured the water over them. There were many too many tea bags, and they weren't Phoebe's favorite Constant Comment, but they'd have to do. I still had a headache. I took the aspirin down from the shelf over the sink and ate a couple.

"That must taste terrible," Will said.

"It does. But whenever I try to swallow pills, I gag." I went into the pantry, got the large everyday serving tray and came back. Then I piled tea pot, mugs, spoons, sugar and milk onto the tray and picked it up.

"Let's go," I said. "We might as well hear Tommy out."

"He has a good case," Will said.

"He has a shitty case," I corrected. "It just happens to be the case he wants. I went over to the hospital today and talked to Damon Rask, you know. He really didn't kill her."

"You like the guy?"

"He's a borderline schizophrenic," I said. "I just know he didn't kill Delia. Or your father. Or my Great-Aunt Felicia, for that matter."

Will gave me an amused look. "Tommy's decided Felicia wasn't murdered after all. He says she did it to herself."

"Suicide? *Felicia?*"

"Accident. Your brother George said she dosed herself with herbal remedies, and Tommy figures she just gave herself a little too much digitalis this last time—"

We were out of the kitchen and into the back hall by then, and the back hall was a cramped and narrow space. I managed to whirl around in it anyway.

"Wait a minute," I said. "Digitalis. Digitalis killed Felicia?" Digitalis came from foxglove. With it, both Tommy and Chris could have what they wanted. Chris could have his prescription overdose that was a form of speed. Digitalis did get prescribed for people and it did speed you up. Tommy could have herbs, and death by accident-on-purpose.

"Delia died of digitalis, too," Will said. That's where Tommy has his problem. *One* person dead of digitalis poisoning is an accident, *two* of them—"

The back hall ended in a swinging door that led to the living room. Will reached over my shoulder and pushed it open for me, chattering all the way.

"You're right, of course," he was saying, "it is a lousy case, but I can't see what else there is to think, under the circumstances, and you can't—"

I stopped listening to him long before he stopped talking. The door was open, and there they all were. Tommy. George. Chris. Elizabeth. Uncle Robert. Phoebe Susanna. Mother. Cordie. Even good old Ephram Aurelius.

Good old Ephram Aurelius. Adopted by my grandfather's brother at the age of five, considered a McKenna for eighty-odd years, until he ended up dead in Uncle Robert's basement and the family wanted to bury him in the McKenna cemetery. And Felicia had protested, because Ephram Aurelius wasn't a McKenna at all.

He was a *Hendershot.* I'd remembered that. I'd just disregarded the obvious. Something definite *had* happened recently. Ephram Aurelius had *died.*

I reached automatically for my cigarettes. My headache was gone, replaced by a floaty feeling that was a little like a trance. Hendershot. Of course the name had sounded familiar. Felicia had made such a big deal out of it just before she died. And of course something out of the ordinary had happened in the last few days. Ephram Aurelius had died.

I got my cigarette lit, and felt a prod between my shoulder blades.

"Patience," Will said. "What's wrong with you? I can't hold this door open forever."

I moved into the living room, slowly, uncomfortably aware that they were all staring at me. Cigarette smoke wound up into my nose, burning the lining. My head had started to ache again. I must have looked on the verge of a conversion experience. Or something.

Mother got out of her chair and came over to me, to take the tray out of my hand.

"Come in and sit down," she said. "You look exhausted."

"She looks sick," George said.

"We've been having a very interesting conversation," Phoebe said. "Tommy Dick was telling us all about Damon and Delia, and I was trying to explain to him how to kill somebody with digitalis, but he wasn't listening to me."

"You were trying to tell him how to kill someone with digitalis?" I said.

"Well, you can find out all about it in a gardening book," Phoebe said. "You just use the leaves to make tea. Then it takes two hours—"

"Two to twenty-four," I said automatically.

"Excuse me?" Tommy Dick said.

"Depending on the dose, it takes two to twenty-four hours for an extract of digitalis to kill somebody," I said.

"I don't see what difference that makes," Tommy Dick said. "It all comes out the same way anyway. Your aunt liked to mix up her own medicines, she got a little careless. Maybe a little forgetful. And Delia had a ton of that stuff in the greenhouse. Foxglove, they call it."

"I know what they call it," I snapped. "Felicia didn't make mistakes. You've got no proof at all that Damon Rask knew a damn thing about foxglove. You're making this all up."

"Patience," my mother said.

"Let me try it," Susanna said. "Patience, you must realize that this is the only thing that makes any sense at all. There couldn't have been any reason for anyone on earth to kill both of them. They barely moved in the same circles. They didn't like each other. You can't just go on and on saying Damon didn't do it. You have to have some idea who did."

"Ah," I said, "I do have some idea. I have a very good idea."

"All right," Susanna said. "Who?"

I looked her straight in the eye and said,

"You."

TWENTY-TWO

IT'S ODD how things like that work out. If this had really been an Ellery Queen novel, she would have jumped up, gone for my throat, raced for the door. She would have done something physical. She would have given herself away. Instead, she just sat there, her eyes getting wider and wider, her body getting very still.

Everybody else just sat there, too. Tommy Dick looked like he thought I'd lost my mind. George had tensed up, not sure what was going to happen if what I'd just said was true. Outside, some sort of precipitation had started falling again. We could hear it knocking against the porch roof and the windows, nature's backbeat. *It was a dark and stormy night.* Oh, dear God, yes. It certainly was that. And Nick was right. I was in the middle of it because I wanted to be in the middle of it. There was no other explanation.

My cigarette had burned into a long column of ash that was threatening to fall onto the carpet. I went to the coffee table and tapped it into the ashtray there. Around me, the crowd was rustling and stirring. The silence had gone on too long, and their examination of me had not produced what they wanted to see. I hadn't lost my mind. I wasn't behaving like Peewee Herman on methamphetamine.

Somebody coughed, and somebody else sneezed. Then Mother said, "Patience, you can't just leave it like that. You can't expect us to believe, with no proof whatsoever, that this perfectly nice young woman killed two people."

"Three," I said. "At least. I haven't decided about Ephram Aurelius yet. I'm not sure it matters."

"Nobody killed Ephram Aurelius," Elizabeth said. "He died in Robert's basement. He'd been killing himself for years."

"I said I wasn't sure it mattered." I put my cigarette out and lit another one. "But there were three murders at least, because you have to count Will Marsh. That's what started it all. That, and the divorce."

Chris stood up. "Stop that. You're not seriously trying to tell me

Susanna went off and killed three people because we got divorced? It was an amicable divorce."

"Would it have been, if she'd had any serious money?"

Chris blinked. "She doesn't have serious money," he said. "She doesn't have any money at all."

"She doesn't have it yet," I said, "but she will. She's the last surviving heir of a man named Hendershot. Hendershot was the original colonial owner of that strip of land between Damon Rask's property and the Deverton place. She wasn't, in 1988. Ephram Aurelius was in the way. Felicia told us he was a Hendershot. But Ephram Aurelius is dead now. And it's all hers. You see, once I knew that piece of land was owned by somebody, it made sense only one way. Somebody had to own it, and somebody had to want to keep that secret. I looked around at all of you, and all I could come up with—the only person I could think of with any reason at all to keep good fortune a secret—was Susanna. She'd want to hold onto that property, Chris. She wouldn't want you to get a piece of the price of it in a divorce."

"But wouldn't that fit me as well as Susanna?" Chris said. "I'm not a monster, but I wasn't giving anything away if I could help it."

"True," I said. "I wouldn't expect you to. But that land would have been worth other things to you besides money. It would have given you something you always wanted, an unassailable membership in an old Waverly family. The oldest, in fact. As far as I can tell, Hendershot was the first one here."

"Christ," Chris said. "Am I really that transparent?"

"Transparent and silly," I told him. "I think you would have given up a little money to get yourself recognized as Hendershot's heir. And you have money, remember. You make a good living. We're not talking about a legendary fortune here. You must make over a hundred thousand a year even now, and you're just starting out."

"But Patience," my father said, "she *wasn't* the owner of that land. If what you say is true, Ephram Aurelius was. And who knows how many relatives there are in the pipeline even now?"

I shrugged. "Ephram Aurelius being alive gave her one more reason to keep the secret. As for the other relatives—she was working in that genealogy place in Morris long before her divorce. She knew her own lineage, and she knew just who was still alive and who wasn't. And there couldn't have been anybody. Ephram Aurelius was adopted because there was no one to take him in, and Susanna's parents died—"

"In 1982," Susanna said tonelessly.

"The Colonial Dames had a dinner at the Red Haddock Inn," I said. "You took Old Will Marsh some dinner on your way out there that night. For some reason, Delia and Felicia were with you—"

"We were all with her," Elizabeth said. "We went out in a stretch."

"All right," I said, "but you don't know anything about plants. Delia and Felicia both did. They knew a lot. I think they saw her put foxglove in the tea or the coffee. They probably didn't realize what was happening. Then later, when Old Will died, they might have remembered it, but they wouldn't have said anything about it. Delia was Susanna's friend. Felicia wouldn't want to bring trouble to a woman of 'good family.' Maybe they didn't even put it together, then. As long as no one knew who owned that property, there was no reason to suspect that Susanna had any reason to murder Old Will Marsh. As soon as the title to that land became clear, there would be."

"You're being ridiculous," Susanna said, suddenly shrill. "Why didn't they stop me at the time? Delia knew everything there was to know about poisonous plants. Why did she let me—"

"I have a guess," I said. "Digitalis isn't an absolute poison. Small amounts of it can be used as a tonic, to help people with heart conditions. They might have thought you were giving Old Will a benign little kick."

"Weak," Susanna said. "Very weak."

"Oh, it's weak enough," I told her. "But I'm right, Susanna. You lied to me, you know. When Phoebe and I came to the bookstore the day we arrived, you told me Felicia hadn't been in. But she had. You admitted to seeing her just a few hours later, just after she died. And she bought a book that day. *The Vanderbilt Era,* by Louis Auchincloss. The charge will be on her American Express card."

"Fine," Susanna said. "How did I talk her into eating a lot of foxglove? You said she'd know what it was."

I had been pacing the length and breadth of the room while I was talking. Now I came to a stop next to Susanna's chair, leaned over, and picked up her Bonwit Teller tote bag. In it was the thermos I'd noticed earlier, when George had been bringing it out to Morris for Susanna's lunch.

"Tea," I said. "You gave Felicia a cup of tea."

"Jesus Christ," Tommy Dick said. "What the *hell*—"

"Oh, shut *up*," Susanna said. She jumped up and grabbed the thermos out of my hand. She was panting and wild. Her hair was suddenly full of sweat. "You can't prove any of this," she said. "You don't know what you're talking about. You were always like this, McKenna. Never interested in a single damn thing but your own importance. You think you're some kind of great detective. You can't let a simple little wife murder alone. It's got to be complicated. It's got to prove you've got a great intellect. I'm not going to let you work your neuroses out on *me*."

"Delia was your best friend," Chris said. "Your *best friend.* For God's sake, Susanna, you'd known her all your life."

"And I'll mourn her all the rest of my life," Susanna said. She stuffed the thermos back into the tote bag, her hands shaking. She was near tears, I could see it, but she was more afraid than anything else. She slung the straps of the tote bag over her shoulder and reached for her coat, left lying over the back of her chair.

"I'm going home now," she said. "If you think you can make anything out of this, you're welcome to try. But I'm going to try, too. I'm not going to let Damon Rask get away with this. And I'm not going to let any of you get away with it either."

"Fine," I said. "Leave the thermos."

"What?"

"Oh dear sweet Jesus," Tommy Dick said.

Susanna was backing toward the door. She was moving very slowly, as if that would hold *us* up. She had pushed the tote bag farther behind her, so that it was hidden behind her back.

"I may be poor these days, McKenna, but I do know lawyers. If you keep this up, I'll sue your ass off."

"Leave the thermos," I said again.

"Consider everything, McKenna. The stakes. The hanging. There was no reason for me to do any of that. There isn't a jury in the world that won't get thrown by everything that's happened in this mess."

"I'm not worried about the jury," I said, "I'm worried about the thermos."

She started to move faster. George, the slowest man on earth in most circumstances, was faster still. He got out of his chair in a single dancer's movement, bent at the waist, and ripped the tote bag off Susanna's arm as easily as if it had been tissue paper.

"This what you want?" he said. "Who was she trying to kill this time?"

"Let me have it," Tommy Dick said. He took it out of George's hands and went looking for a jacket pocket big enough to hold it. He didn't have one. "Dear sweet Jesus Christ," he said again. "What the hell has gotten into everybody?"

"Is that thing really full of digitalis?" Chris said. "Was she really going to off somebody else? Who could she possibly want dead now?"

"My guess," I said, "would be you. Just in case you wanted to take her back to court, maybe. Or just in case you know something you don't know you know yet. You're a doctor. You gave the death certificate on Felicia. Did you give the death certificate on Old Will Marsh?"

"Yeah," Chris said. "I did."

"You'd know something about poisons, Chris."

Susanna started to giggle. "Oh God," she said. "This is funny. This is so funny I can't stand it. Kill Chris. Kill Chris, for God's sake. Oh God, you dumb oversized bitch. You think you know everything." She turned to Chris. "Let me tell you something," she said. "If you're going to murder somebody, always murder a friend. It's the easiest hit." Then she turned back to me. "That," she said, pointing at the thermos, "was meant for *you.*"

EPILOGUE

ON THE DAY I WAS MARRIED, Adrienne, Courtney Feinberg and my niece Andrea spent the morning in my room, grilling me. Phoebe and my mother were there, too, but they were occupied with other things. Phoebe was feeling funny again. My mother was in a state of collapse because I was so much thinner than her mother's mother had been. It was her mother's mother's wedding dress I was wearing for the ceremony. I would have worn hers, but hers was white. That much of a hypocrite, I couldn't be. My great-grandmother's dress was pale pink. I thought that said it all.

I had put the dress on and taken it off again for the fifth time when Adrienne brought up what had been on her mind all weekend—or maybe all of the year and some odd months since her mother had been murdered. She approached me very solemnly, with Courtney and Andrea to back her up. I knew from the looks on their faces that it was time I really listened.

"Patience," she said, "do you believe in God?"

I had been expecting something else. To be precise, I had been expecting sex, and I had my answers all ready for the first round of questions about the Facts of Life. But Adrienne was Adrienne, and Courtney and Andrea tended to follow her lead. She wasn't worried about Facts as much as she was about Meaning.

And I, of course, had no answers to questions about meaning.

Phoebe had gone to the bathroom. Mother had gone to find a spool of pink silk thread. I sat down on the bed and reached for my cigarettes. Three pairs of eyes squinted at me, willing me to quit.

"Well," I said. "Um. Huh. What brought this up?"

There was a quick conference—three very small people with IQ's in the two hundreds trying to think of a way to make the stupid grown-up *understand.* Adrienne came back and said,

"Courtney is Jewish. Andrea is Catholic. I'm Episcopalian in the city, but you're getting married in a Congregational Church."

"Right," I said.

"Well," Andrea said, "do you believe in God? Are you getting married in church so you can promise God to stay married? And how do you know if you're in the right church? And—"

"What we really want to know," Courtney said, "is if there's a God there somewhere who'll punish that lady. The one that Mr. Carras was —um—talking about."

I understood the "um." Since coming up to Connecticut, Nick had not been "talking" about the murders. He'd been swearing. On the Saturday after Susanna was arrested, he'd managed to use the *f*-word fifteen times in twenty-two seconds.

He beat that record two days later, this past Monday, when it turned out that, arrested or not, Susanna was not going to be tried. She'd changed her tack after she'd been booked. She'd become very calm, and very normal. As soon as she got Tommy Dick into a relaxed state, she managed to steal the thermos. And drink it.

She didn't die of it, because they knew what they were dealing with. She did, however, get rid of most of the evidence. There were traces, but not enough for the prosecutor's office. Tommy had kept a lid on that one for almost a week, but it had to come out sometime, and it finally did. It wasn't making any of us happy.

I fished the ashtray out of my night table drawer and dumped my cigarette into it. "Actually," I said, "what I figure is, if there's a God, he punishes criminals in advance."

"In advance?" Adrienne said.

"Yeah," I said. "In fact, now that I think of it, that must mean there is a God, because it almost always works out that way. Every murderer I ever knew was stupid. Not just stupid about one thing, the thing they got caught on, but about lots of things. As far as I can figure out, you have to be stupid to commit murder to begin with."

"I don't know," Courtney said, "that thing with the thermos was pretty smart."

"Except that it landed her in the hospital and got her stomach pumped and could have killed her," I said. "And now what?"

"Well, that's just the point, isn't it?" Adrienne said. "Now what? If they don't try her, they'll have to let her go. She can just get on with her life as if she'd never done any of those things."

"Not exactly. I don't think Damon Rask is going to buy that piece of land from her. He's crazy, but he's not that crazy. And the

Deverton place won't be settled for God only knows how long. That strip of land is completely worthless at the moment. She won't get the money she wanted. And she won't last long at that job of hers, either. It might take them a little while, but they'll get rid of her."

"She could move someplace else," Andrea said.

"She could. But what would she do when she got there? She's got a degree from Bennington in some kind of creative arts, but she has no experience actually doing anything. She's worked in a bookstore and she's worked as a clerk. I'm certainly not going to help her get a job in New York, not now. What do you figure she's going to do for money?"

"She could get married," Adrienne said.

"Not around here," I said. "And not to what Great-Aunt Felicia would have called 'a member of her own class.' Good old cousin Elizabeth will have this story all over the society circuit by Easter. If she hasn't managed to spread it yet."

"But *Patience,*" Adrienne said.

"I'm not saying it wouldn't be better if they found some way to put her in jail," I said. "I'm just saying she's not going to get absolutely away with it."

"I don't think that tells me whether there's a God or not," Adrienne said.

I rumpled her hair a little. "I hate to tell you this, but I think every one of us is going to have to die and find out for ourselves."

The three of them looked at each other, and then subsided on the bed. My mother came in, did something to the dress, and held it in the air for me to get under.

"Beautiful," she said, when I finally had it on. "Oh, Patience. I really never thought I'd see you married. You're just the most unlikely woman—"

"To get married?"

"Like your father's Great-Aunt Magdalen. The one who ran away to Turkey and lived in a cave with a hookah for thirty years."

I decided to leave my father's Great-Aunt Magdalen out of this. I sucked in my stomach so the zipper would go up, then bent over to let Mother fasten the veil on my head. Now that I was actually wearing the thing, it didn't feel so bad. I was even willing to admit that Mother may have had a point. Getting married in full regalia does give a solemnity to the occasion a quickie ceremony in City Hall would have lacked. I bent over to get a look at myself in the mirror, then turned around to check out the girls.

The girls were wearing old-rose velvet jumpers and high-necked silk blouses and little circlets of flowers in their hair. The clothes had been made to order at one of my mother's secret "places" in the city. They had probably cost umpteen-hundreds of dollars, but I wasn't going to worry about that. I wasn't going to worry about anything. My status as an intended murder victim had produced a sea change in my mother. She'd left me absolutely alone since the night Susanna was taken out of our house in handcuffs. I'd had almost two weeks to relax and read, and seven days to spend with Nick. I'd have spent them with Adrienne, too, but she was too busy cooking things up with Andrea and Courtney. She and Courtney hadn't been out to the country in a while.

Phoebe came back from the bathroom, and I got Mother's lambswool stole off the bed to throw around my shoulders.

"Nick safely out of the house?" I asked.

"At the church already," Adrienne promised.

"Everybody get here?"

"The romance writers certainly did," Phoebe said, sounding strangled. "Amelia's carrying around a five-pound bag of birdseed to use instead of rice, and Tempesta Stewart is telling everyone who'll listen how this is going to be the day you speak in tongues."

"Just as long as Cordie doesn't speak in tongues," I said, "I'll be satisfied. Let's go."

Mother stepped back and gave me a funny look. I thought I recognized it. It was the same one she'd given me when I first emerged from the womb.

"Are you sure, Patience?"

"Very sure," I said.

"All right."

"You'd better put your sunglasses on, Grandmama," Adrienne said. "You're leaking."

She was, indeed, leaking. So was I. I took her arm and we went out of the room, down the hall, down the stairs to the foyer. My father was there, and he was leaking, too. I took his arm in my other hand and we went out to the car.

Coming into town, I found the wedding had caused a traffic jam. There were cars parked along every inch of curb, taking up every

square foot of parking space, blocking every driveway. Will Marsh
was standing in front of the church, uncomfortable in a rented tuxedo,
trying to keep people from double-parking directly in front of the
church doors. *We* were supposed to double-park there.

We did, and I got out, and the first thing I saw was Nick, standing at
the top of the steps. The sick look on his face cleared almost as soon as
he saw me—as if he'd been afraid I wouldn't show up. He should have
known he had Mother on his side. If I'd shown the least inclination to
back down, she would have killed me.

I got out of the car, lifted my train above the snow, and looked
around. There had been a decent fall the night before. What was on
the ground was fresh and white. The sky was clear. The streets were
full of Litchfield County Ladies—in good silk shirtwaists now, as befit-
ted a wedding. I waved to Cassie and Ellen, going into the church with
anonymous men in tow. They waved back.

I was turning back to the car to make sure Phoebe was all right
when I saw her. She was sitting on the steps of a tall white house
whose owners were probably already in their pew. She was wearing
jeans and a sweater and a rough denim jacket, and she was staring
straight at me.

Susanna Mars.

The first thing that came into my head was: *I wonder how it would
have all turned out if Old Will Marsh hadn't been so fussy about those stakes.*
Fussiness was why he had had them with him, and having them with
him was what had tipped off Tommy Dick that something out of the
ordinary was going on. Young Willie had figured that out for us later.
Old Will had been putting the stakes where they ought to be, if you
surveyed the land from within the strip instead of outside it.

"Patience?"

My mother had hold of my arm. I turned away from Susanna and let
Mother lead me up to the church door, chattering and nattering all the
way. When we got inside, she left me in the vestibule with Phoebe
and my father and the girls, to take her place with the other mothers in
the front pew. At most weddings, there is a bride's side and a groom's
side. At this one, tradition was being scrapped for the sake of camara-
derie. Nick's mother was an immigrant from Greece. Phoebe's
mother was a survivor of the Holocaust. My mother was a New England aristocrat. You wouldn't *believe* how much those three women
had to say to each other.

Daddy crooked his arm, and I slipped my hand through. Somewhere inside, the music started up, fortunately *not* the wedding march from Lohengrin. I took a deep breath and said, "Okay. Let's go."

"Are you happy, Patience?" my father asked me.

"Very happy. About almost everything."

He looked toward the church door. "I could go ask her to move," he said. "I don't know if it would do any good."

"I'm a very bad person, Daddy. I don't want her to move."

"Good girl."

After that, there would have been nothing left but the wedding itself—but my life is never that simple.

Never.

And although I didn't know until I got to the reception, I should have realized before I ever started walking down the aisle of that church.

Phoebe was in labor.

Orania Papazoglou lives in Watertown, Connecticut, and is a Litchfield County Lady. She has a husband, a son, a cat, and one of those old houses where the plumbing speaks Chinese. Frequently. *Once and Always Murder* is her fifth novel for the Crime Club.

DISCARD